eleven

TOM ROGERS

Alto Nido Press
Los Angeles

DEDICATION

This book is dedicated to those who perished in the attacks of September 11, 2001, and to all the courageous first responders, supporters, survivors, volunteers, families, neighbors, and communities who came together in this tragedy and showed us all the better angels of our nature.

CHAPTER 1
A-Dawg

Monday. 5:39 p.m.

All his life, A-Dawg had wanted to be a hero.

Now, his time had come.

Five seconds ago, A-Dawg had been seated squarely in the cockpit of his F-16, guiding it with ease as it knifed through the air.

Then everything changed.

The enemy plane came out of nowhere. A-Dawg reacted on pure instinct. The missile clipped his wing as he pulled up hard on the yoke and rolled into an inverted dive that flipped the horizon over, putting the buildings above and the sky below and turning his whole world upside down.

The daredevil maneuver worked. When he straightened out, he'd lost his pursuer.

He was trailing smoke and leaking fuel. He checked his gauges. If he tucked his tail and ran away, he'd have just enough juice to make it back to base.

Or he could make the ultimate sacrifice and do what had to be done.

He glanced at a photo of his dog, tucked into the instrument panel. The dog gazed back, loyal, proud, and brave. Maybe it was his mind playing tricks, the G forces sloshing his brain around, but A-Dawg was sure he saw his dog nod.

A-Dawg knew what he had to do.

He banked sharply and swung back into the fight. He was face-to-face with the enemy plane across a three-mile gap, on a collision course and closing fast. He brought the crosshairs into focus on his target. A tone sounded: radar lock.

Then a voice crackled in his headset. *"Okay, hotshot, time's up. Bring it in."*

"Not yet. I have a job to do."

"You know the rules."

A-Dawg knew the rules. But today, the rules went out the window.

His glove tightened on the stick. His thumb brushed the red firing button.

The other plane fired first.

"FIRE!" A-Dawg stabbed his thumb down. His airplane shook as a missile leapt off the wing, riding a trail of flame. A-Dawg banked away, straining to see behind him. Did he get the job done? Was he about to be a hero?

He twisted in the cockpit, desperate to see what happened.

And then everything went black.

CHAPTER 2
The Home Front

Monday. 5:40 p.m.

Alex Douglas frowned at the darkened computer. He toggled the joystick, stabbed at the keyboard, hit the red firing button. Nothing. Dead. Then he saw her in the reflection on the screen, like a white-robed ghost, arms folded.

"MOoooooOOM!" he groaned, gritting his teeth.

Alex's mother loomed over him in her white nurse's uniform. She had just come off a twelve-hour shift at Mercy Hospital in Jersey City and was in no mood for guff. She narrowed her eyes and pointed at him with the flopping end of the computer plug she'd just yanked out of the wall, totally crashing his Screaming Eagles IV flight-sim game in the middle of what would have been his most heroic victory EVER. He was about to save the world, but he hadn't even had time to hit "save."

"God, Mom, how can you be so STUPID???"

He didn't really say that out loud. But he thought it so loudly he was afraid she might hear it echoing in his brain. If he had said it out loud, he probably wouldn't have lived to see his eleventh birthday (only seven hours and fifty-one minutes away, he calculated).

Alex had discovered over the years that he wasn't so great at hiding his thoughts from his parents. Lately, he'd been practicing in front of the mirror, thinking of stuff that made him mad while trying to keep his feelings from showing on his face. He was pretty sure he was getting better at it.

"Don't give me that look," said his mom. "I know what you're thinking."

Guess there's still room for improvement, he thought.

"What are the rules?" she asked.

Alex spotted movement out of the corner of his eye.

"Rule 1: Nunu has to stay on her side of the flight line."

Alex pointed at his six-year-old sister, who was

about to cross a black-and-yellow stripe that Alex had taped on the floor, dividing the room in two. Nunu (her real name was Nolabeth, but everyone called her Nunu) sighed and flopped back onto her bed. Everything on her side of the room was pink: pink bed, pink princess sheets, pink dolls piled up on pink pillows. Even the walls on her side were painted the color of shiny, chewed bubble gum. Alex had one word for it.

Gross.

The other side of the room, Alex's side, was made of awesome. He had turned it into a shrine to the two things he loved: airplanes and dogs. Four airplane models dangled from the ceiling on strings: a huge Boeing 747, a World War II-era P-51 Mustang (its nose painted to look like a shark's mouth), a Sopwith Camel biplane, and an F-16 Fighting Falcon, exactly like the one he was flying before his mother pulled the plug on his computer. He'd even stenciled his own call-sign, "A-Dawg," onto the nose of the fighter jet. Posters of airplanes covered the walls. Over his bed, tacked to the ceiling, was a huge fold-out of a 747 cockpit; staring up at it night after night before bed, he'd memorized the location and function of every single dial and switch.

On his dresser sat a framed photograph of the Navy's Blue Angels elite flying squadron in close formation, signed by every pilot on the team. He got that for his birthday two years ago, when his dad took him to an air show in upstate New York. They'd gotten up super early, way before dawn, and even though he was dog-tired because he'd hardly slept the night before, he was wide awake by the time they pulled onto the air base and parked in a field near the viewing stand. It was so early the bleachers were still wet with dew – not that it mattered, because he never once sat down.

He remembered every detail and maneuver like it had happened yesterday. Even his dad seemed impressed. Alex's dad drove a commuter train for a living, which meant he was in charge of steering a half-million pounds of steel and aluminum through a tunnel underneath the Hudson River at seventy miles per hour, so it took a lot to impress him. In the air show finale, the Angels flew low and fast right over the crowd, four fighter jets in a tight diamond pattern, so close overhead that Alex felt like he could reach out and touch their wings. He could still remember how the roar of the engines made his insides rumble.

Right after the Angels flew past, Alex's dad reached down and squeezed his shoulder. Alex looked up, his fingers still in his ears to dull the roar of the jets. His dad grinned at him and mouthed one word:

"WOW."

He had always thought of that day as his Greatest Birthday Ever.

Until this one. This one was going to leave that year's in the—

"Alex, answer the question."

Alex froze. He'd totally forgotten what they were talking about.

"I asked you about the rules," she reminded him.

"You didn't say *which* rules."

"Careful, young man."

Ugh. He hated when she called him "young man." The fact that it had the word *man* in it didn't really help, because the only word that mattered was *young*. *Man* was like those silent letters they'd just learned about in English class, like the *s* in *island* or the *g* in *phlegm*. He thought of it as a new part of speech: the silent *man*.

His mom and dad were always telling him he needed to grow up. It was one of the things he definitely agreed with them about. Because if growing up meant getting better at hiding your feelings so you don't get in trouble, then he was all for it. He wondered if he'd be better at it once he turned eleven.

All he knew for sure was that growing up meant he could get a dog.

And that's why this was going to be his official new Greatest Birthday Ever.

He'd been asking for a dog since forever. Last year, his parents said they'd think about getting him a dog when he was old enough to take care of one. That was all the encouragement he needed. Six months ago, he'd started his campaign, dropping hints, a steady stream of little reminders that built and built into a tidal wave. Post-its with the number of days to his birthday would mysteriously appear on his parents' bathroom mirror. Pictures of dogs would turn up inside their favorite magazines or stuck to the refrigerator door. At two months out, he turned it up another notch, beginning almost every sentence with, "When I get a dog...." "*If* you get a dog," his parents would correct him. But he was relentless, and before long they stopped saying "If" and would just trade exasperated looks. That's how he knew it was finally happening; he'd worn them down.

He was definitely getting a dog for his birthday.

Which explained the other half of Alex's half of the room.

The other half of Alex's half of the room was plastered with pictures of dogs. Everywhere there wasn't an airplane, there was a dog. To Alex, airplanes and dogs went together like peanut butter and baloney, which happened to be his favorite sandwich. When he wasn't playing flight-sim or memorizing cockpit dials or throwing dirty socks at Nunu to keep her on her side of the flight line, he'd stare at all the pictures and daydream about how cool it would be if a dog could fly a pla—

"Alex Douglas, pay attention!"

First AND last name. He was in the danger zone now.

"What are the rules? And this time, I expect a straight answer."

Alex sighed. "No games until my homework is done."

"And?"

"And my chores."

"And are they done?"

"Define 'done.'"

Dead silence. Alex withered slightly, then rebounded. He could usually get out of a tough spot by making his mother laugh.

"How do you know that time travel isn't possible and I didn't just time-warp two hours into the past, do my chores, and then time-warp right back into my chair?"

"Call it maternal instinct."

But he thought he saw her crack a tiny smile.

Across the room, Nunu giggled. Despite the dirty socks, she always laughed at her brother's dumb jokes.

If it weren't for Nunu's Lolly doll, Alex might have been willing to overlook her other flaws, like her pink sheets or her very existence on this planet (especially the part of the planet that included the other half of *his* bedroom). But she never went anywhere without Lolly. And by the time you counted the bus ride to school every day, the bus ride home, and anywhere they went with their parents, Alex felt like he never went anywhere without *Nunu*. Which meant that he never went anywhere without Lolly and her missing eye and that one ear Nunu had chewed on until it was practically gone, worn down to a hard, spit-dark, threadbare nub.

Lolly had ruined his life.

It happened the first week of school. Nunu was halfway onto the bus when she whirled around and pointed: she'd left Lolly on the bench. Alex sighed but sprinted back off the bus and snatched up the soggy-eared doll.

Just as Jordan McCreevey sauntered up.

Jordan the Jerk.

That's what Alex and his friends called him behind his back. If they'd ever called him that to his face, they probably wouldn't have faces anymore.

Jordan snatched the pink doll out of Alex's hand. Alex made a half-hearted attempt to take it back, but Jordan held it way up high, out of reach, as he stared down at Alex. The left side of his mouth began to curl. Alex flinched as Jordan laughed in his face; his breath stank like armpit and Cheetos. Then Jordan slapped the doll onto Alex's head like a dunce cap.

"Here's your baby...baby."

And that's when Alex knew that Jordan McCreevey was going to make his life a living hell.

"Alex." His mom again.

"What? I'm listening."

"Really. Okay, I'll make you a deal. Answer one easy question for me, and you can have ten more minutes on the computer. Fair?"

Alex's eyebrows shot up. He liked where this was going. He was constantly trying to make deals with his parents to get out of doing stuff right away. "Please, just five more minutes, and then I promise I'll do the dishes," he'd beg, and then they'd forget the time limit, five minutes would become twenty, and half the time the dishes would get done while he was away. But this was a new twist: now his mom was offering *him* a deal. Sweet.

"Fire away," he said with confidence.

"Here's the question: what were we just talking about?"

Alex opened his mouth, then shut it. Uh-oh. He frowned and saw where he'd messed up: he was a daydreamer. And she knew it. His mind had a tendency to wander. Like this one time last week in

Ms. Foster's room, when they were supposed to be doing class participation, but then he saw this dog run by outside the window—

"That's what I thought." His mom shook her head and started for the kitchen. "Now leave that computer off, take out your books, and do your homework."

She was halfway across the living room when Alex bolted into the hall.

"HOMEWORK!" he shouted triumphantly.

His mom laughed. But she wasn't buying it.

"Please, Mom? Ten more minutes—"

"No."

"Five? And I'll do the dishes."

"No more deal-making."

"But it's my birthday tomorrow," he wheedled.

"I know. That's why you have to get your homework done today."

Alex tried a different tack. "You know what, Mom? You're absolutely right. That is so smart. I really should get ahead on my homework."

His mother cocked an eyebrow, wondering where this was going.

"That way I'll have more time to play with the dog you're getting me for my birthday."

"Alex—"

"You promised. You promised I could get a dog for my birthday—"

"I know, sweetie. *If* you got serious about your schoolwork. And *if* your grades improved. But you got a C on your last math test."

"Yeah, but look on the bright side. At least you know I didn't cheat."

He grinned, hoping he could get a smile out of her.

She shook her head. "We talked about this. A dog is a big responsibility. And you have to show us you can handle that kind of responsibility."

"Responsibility? Are you kidding me? I can land an F/A-18 Hornet on an aircraft carrier in a rolling sea! If you can trust me with a 30 million dollar airplane, I think you can trust me with a dog."

His Mom didn't laugh.

"Mom! You promised. What do I have to do?"

"Your homework."

Then she turned and headed into the kitchen.

Alex stared after her, a sick feeling growing in his stomach.

Maybe he wasn't getting a dog after all.

When his mom called him to dinner, Alex headed downstairs. He'd finished his homework, which was pretty easy (some long division and fractions and a chapter on the American Revolution with only four study questions). But even though nothing put him in a good mood faster than easy homework, he couldn't shake the feeling that his plans for the Greatest Birthday Ever were falling apart like a bad game of Jenga.

He drifted into the living room, scuffing his feet along the carpet, headed for the worn Barcalounger next to the old gray sofa in front of the TV. As usual, he took the shortcut, stepping from arm to arm of the lounge chair and then vaulting over the back of the sofa. As he landed, he froze. He turned back, staring at the worn lounge chair. His dad's chair. Then it came to him, the way to get around his mom:

Talk to Dad.

Nunu and their mother were already sitting when Alex came in. He grabbed the back of his chair and dragged it out from under the table, like he'd been told a thousand times not to, but never remembered. The legs made a loud, honking noise as they scraped across the linoleum. His mother shot him a look. Uh-oh, he thought. Don't jinx it. He stopped with the chair halfway out, then tried to squeeze noiselessly into his seat. The table shook; milk splashed out of Nunu's glass. Rats.

"Sorry," he mumbled.

His mom dabbed up the spill. "Drink your milk, honey," she said to Nunu.

Dinner was hot dogs, macaroni and cheese, and

carrots. His mom had made his favorite meal (except for the carrots). This was a good sign.

"Where's Daddy?" Nunu asked.

"They gave him an extra run, so he'll be home a little late."

Another good sign. It gave him more time to plan his charm offensive.

Alex could feel his mom watching him. He was still sort of mad at her and didn't want to look her in the eye, but he knew he'd better straighten up and fly right if he had any chance of saving the Greatest Birthday Ever. He took a huge bite of hot dog and turned to his mom with a big smile.

"Grrrt httt dgggg, Mmm."

"Don't talk with your mouth full," she said. But then she smiled.

Alex could feel the tide turning in his favor.

An hour later, Alex was sitting up in bed, English book propped in his lap and a brand new plan taking shape in his brain. Plan A was to talk to his dad. But Alex figured you can never be too safe, so when he came back up to his room, he made a back-up deal with the universe: if I stop thinking about dogs and do my homework, then I'll be rewarded with a dog.

Alex was always making deals with the universe.

In the morning: "If I actually brush my teeth instead of just waving the brush around like a light saber, then Mom will have pancakes on the table." In fifth period: "If I don't look at the clock for five minutes, class will end early." Once in a while, it worked ("If I sit perfectly still, Jordan won't see me"), and that was all Alex needed to make him believe.

But even with Plan A in place and Plan B as backup, he couldn't shake the feeling that this wasn't going to end well.

Deep down, he knew what was really bugging him and why he was in such an up-and-down mood. His mother was right: it was his own fault he wasn't getting a dog. They'd made a straightforward deal, just like the ones he made with the universe: improve your grades, and you can have a dog. But he'd dropped the ball, and now he had nobody to blame but himself, which made it even worse, like when you stub your toe and you want to scream and yell at someone but you can't, because that someone is you.

So here he was, on the eve of his birthday, trying not to think about dogs.

He'd been staring at the same page for five minutes before he realized that the words were just a blur and that his mind had wandered back to dogs. He shook his head and tried to focus. But the harder he tried, the more he thought about dogs. It was impossible not to think of dogs, and it was driving him crazy.

"Daddy!" Nunu's happy voice penetrated the thin walls.

"C'mere, monkey!" boomed his father.

Alex sat up straight with his English book and forced a studious look onto his face. They'd see he'd changed. They'd see he deserved a dog after all.

They'd see right through him in a second.

Who was he kidding? It was too little, too late. His mood came crashing down again as he shoved the book aside, turned off the light, and rolled over to face the wall, feeling sorry for himself. Maybe they'd feel sorry for him, too.

Lying in darkness, his back to the room, he pricked up his ears as the door opened with a click. A sliver of light spilled in from the hallway.

"Shhh. Looks like he's asleep." His father's voice.

"No, he's not. He's faking it," said Nunu, riding on their father's shoulders.

Alex clamped his eyes shut. He didn't need to see to know what was going on. It was the same routine every night. The pink sheets rustled as his father lowered Nunu into her bed.

"Sing 'No Deer' Daddy."

Alex groaned and rolled over, pulling a pillow

over his head. "I hate that stupid song," came his muffled voice.

"He sure is a Grumpy Gus," said their father.

"Grumpy Alex," Nunu replied.

Their father stroked Nunu's hair and began to sing.

Alex tried to drown them out, but either the pillow wasn't thick enough, or he knew the routine too well.

"You are my sunshine, my only sunshine

"You make me happy, when skies are gray.

"You'll never—"

"No Deer!" He knew it was coming, but Alex still winced as Nunu sang out her favorite line, just like she did every single solitary stupid night. As usual, she messed up the words. Most of the time, he didn't notice it anymore. But now it bugged him. Why does she get to mess up every night, and I don't? Even as he thought it, he knew it wasn't the same thing, but it was the best he could do on short notice.

"How much I love you.

"Please don't take my sunshine away."

Nunu snuggled down into her comforter. Alex heard her breathing slow as their dad stroked her hair and she gradually drifted off to sleep.

The bed creaked as his dad sat down beside him. For a long time, his father said nothing. Peering through the crack under his pillow, Alex could see bits and pieces of his father: the heel of his left shoe, worn down so far it curved underneath; the light from the hallway reflecting off a shiny spot on his pants knee, where the crease in the fabric just seemed to disappear; two loose threads standing straight up off the cuff of his stark white shirt.

Alex felt his father's hand land gently on his shoulder.

"Tower to A-Dawg. Come in, A-Dawg."

A-Dawg maintained radio silence.

"Mom told me you two went 'round and 'round. Everything okay at school?"

"Who cares about school?" Under the pillow, Alex rolled his eyes.

"School's important—"

"It's not school. School's fine."

"Is this about the dog?"

Alex felt a flicker of hope. His dad knew how much this meant to him. He held his breath and waited, afraid to say anything that might wreck his chances.

His dad gently tugged the pillow down.

"Why do you want a dog so badly?"

A thousand answers popped into Alex's head. He shrugged.

"You had a dog when you were growing up."

His dad smiled. Good, thought Alex.

"Yeah. Rufus."

"What kind was he?"

"More like, what kind wasn't he. Not much to look at, but he was a great dog."

"I bet."

"He used to sit in the front window every day with a stick in his mouth and wait for me to come home from school to play fetch."

"Wow."

They smiled together.

"How old were you when you got him?" Alex asked.

His dad looked him in the eye. "Old enough to take care of him."

Alex collapsed inside.

"I can take care of a dog."

"Your dog has to be able to count on you."

"I *know*."

"Taking care of a dog is a big responsibility."

Alex felt a surge of panic. It was all slipping away.

"I AM responsible. I'm gonna be eleven. Way into double digits."

"It's not just about age, Alex. It's about acting more grown up."

Alex shot straight up. "I AM ACTING LIKE A GROWN UP!"

Then he flopped down and yanked the pillow

back over his head.

His dad tried to pat him on the shoulder, but Alex jerked away and rolled over to face the wall. His dad exhaled heavily, then rubbed his eyes and stood.

"If you loved me, you'd get me a dog," said Alex.

His father paused at the door, his hand resting on the handle.

"I do love you, Alex."

His dad waited. The silence seemed to stretch on endlessly.

"I hate you," came the quiet reply from the bed.

Then Alex heard the door click shut.

CHAPTER 3
Man in the Mirror

Tuesday. 7:02 a.m.

When Alex woke up the next morning, he was eleven.

Simple as that.

He rolled out of bed and hustled down the hall to the bathroom. He was in a hurry not only because he had to pee like a race horse, but also because he was dying to get to the mirror and see if he looked any older.

Alex gazed at his reflection for a very long time.

Yup. Definitely older. Probably start shaving soon, he thought.

Like Dad.

Alex remembered what he'd said to his father last night. He replayed it in his head, trying to convince himself that he'd said it so quietly, under his breath, that maybe his dad hadn't heard.

He shook it off, trying to get the good feeling back. In the bright light of a new day, his mom and dad's resistance to getting a dog made perfect sense: it had to be a trick to throw him off the scent. Of COURSE they would pretend he wasn't getting a dog; otherwise, it wouldn't be a surprise.

Back in his room, Alex quickly tugged on pants and a shirt, suddenly anxious to get out there. He moved so fast that he yanked the shirt on backwards, the tag in front, and had to pull his arms in and twist it around to get it on straight. He jammed on his Heelys and sped down the hall, pulling up cautiously outside the kitchen. After last night's blow up, he had his radar on, checking for signs. Then he noticed the smell of pancakes. His favorite. Mom cooked his favorite dinner last night and his favorite breakfast today. Would she really do that if she were trying to punish him—or deny him his one birthday wish?

Alex breezed into the kitchen on his Heelys, arms out wide like airplane wings. He spun to a stop, flopped into his chair, and guzzled his o.j., draining the glass in three gulps. His mom stood at the sink washing dishes, half-watching the morning show on a tiny TV propped on the counter. His father's chair was pushed in, his plate gone.

"Where's Dad?" he asked, banging the empty juice glass down.

"Good morning to you, too," she answered. There was a smile in her voice. A good sign.

He grinned. "Morning, Mom. Where's Dad?"

"He had the early run today."

Alex sank a little. He'd been hoping to get a read on his dad this morning.

"Hey. How'd I do?"

His mom stood beside him holding a huge chocolate cake on a tray. Chocolate fudge icing covered the entire cake, with a ribbon of chocolate icing around the edge. "Tower to A-Dawg: Happy Birthday!!!" was written in green on top. There was even an icing airplane flying across the cake.

"Whoa," said Alex.

She smiled and kissed him on the head. "Happy birthday, Sweetie."

"Mom, don't call me Sweetie!" he laughed. But he didn't really mind.

"I'm your mother, so I get to call you whatever I want. Sweetie."

He reached out with his finger to swipe at the icing. But she was too quick.

"Ah-ah! This is for tonight." She pointed to a bakery box full of cupcakes, one for everybody in his homeroom. "Those are for school."

"Awesome."

Nunu stumbled into the kitchen, sleepy-eyed, and flopped into her chair. As she drank her orange juice, she noticed the cake.

"Happy birthday, Alex," she mumbled, her voice echoing inside her juice glass.

Alex's mom slid a plate of steaming hot pancakes in front of him. As he drowned them in butter and syrup, he decided that last night had just been a hitch. His parents were trying to surprise him, he'd pushed too hard, and he'd somehow gotten into a stupid fight with his dad. But now everything seemed to be okay.

The Greatest Birthday Ever was back on track.

"Alex, you're going to miss the bus!"

His mom gave the school bus driver an apologetic wave. The driver, a sour-faced woman named Mary Jo, responded by honking again. Alex finally appeared at the door, hoisting his enormous backpack on with a grunt. His mom handed him the bakery box full of cupcakes.

"Now look. No eating these on the bus. These are for your party in homeroom at lunch. Got it?"

"Of course, Mom," he answered with excessive politeness. "I would never do something so immature."

"Okay."

"I will take responsibility for these cupcakes. Now that I'm eleven, I can handle that kind of responsibility. If there's one thing I am, it's responsible."

"Don't go there, Alex."

"I'm even responsible enough to take care of a dog."

"You're definitely persistent."

"That's like responsible, right?"

"You'll miss your bus."

She's taking this game pretty far, he thought to himself.

Then he noticed she wasn't looking at him. She was avoiding eye contact. And nothing about her expression looked like she was playing a game.

All of his confidence evaporated. They weren't playing games. They weren't stringing him along, holding off a big surprise.

They really weren't going to get him a dog.

CHAPTER 4
You Smell Like a Monkey

8:05 a.m.

"So what do you want for your birthday?" asked Kwan.

"Fly jets. Get a dog," answered two voices in unison.

Alex looked over as Doug said the words along with him.

"Same as always." Doug busted him.

"You're totally bogus, same as always," Alex laughed.

Alex was twisted around in his school bus seat, talking to his two best friends in the row behind him. Kwan was tall and skinny, with big ears that stuck out like handles from his smallish head, which sat atop a neck like a giraffe's; his straight black hair was cut short, so it stood up on top in a tuft of bristles, adding to the impression he ate his meals out of a basket on a pole.

Doug got the triple whammy: glasses, braces, pimples.

"Anyway, kids can't fly jets," said Kwan.

"Says who?" Alex shot back.

"Says the whole world."

"I can land an FA-18 Hornet—"

"—on the back of an aircraft carrier in thirty-foot seas," Kwan and Doug said in unison. They'd heard it a thousand times.

"News flash: it's a video game," said Doug.

"News flash: you're still bogus," Alex replied.

"DOUGLAS! TURN AROUND!"

Doug and Alex both snapped their heads up— Doug because his full name was Douglas (which nobody called him except when he was in trouble), and Alex because that was his last name. Mary Jo, the world's angriest bus driver, glared at Alex in the rearview mirror. Doug let out a sigh of relief when he realized she wasn't talking to him.

"Alex Douglas, turn around and SIT DOWN," she repeated.

Alex felt his ears go red as he sat down and faced forward. All the other kids on the bus were facing backwards, staring at him. Why didn't she tell *them* to turn around?

Some birthday, he thought.

The yellow bus rumbled through a tumbledown section of town, an industrial no-man's-land of railroad tracks, warehouses, and empty factories with broken windows and rusted steel roofs. The bus didn't stop here, because no kids lived here.

The sound of the tires changed to a high-pitched hum as the bus crossed a tall bridge that soared over a rail yard and a narrow river. Alex turned to look out the window. From the highest point of the bridge, he could see over the rooftops of Jersey City, all the way to the tall towers of the Manhattan skyline, poking up like the teeth of a comb in the distance.

Alex loved that view. And he loved thinking about his dad, somewhere out there under the Hudson River, driving his PATH train to the World Trade Center.

The bus descended the other side of the bridge. Manhattan disappeared for good.

"Yo, A-Dawg. Check it out." It was Kwan, behind him.

Alex glanced up to see if Mary Jo was looking, but her eyes were on the traffic. The brakes squealed as she pulled over to pick up more kids. Alex turned sideways in his seat. Kwan held up his Gameboy.

"I broke 8 million."

"Dude." Alex and Kwan slid palms in an elaborate high-five: up, down, side-to-side, then a bump-bump to finish.

"Mayday mayday. Bogeys at twelve," Doug interrupted, under his breath.

Alex turned—and came face to face with the sneering mug of Calvin Butts.

Calvin Butts was one of Jordan McCreevey's two goons. All three were a grade ahead of Alex. Calvin jerked his head, and the boy in front of Alex scrambled to a different row. Calvin slammed his squat, square, heavy body into the seat and stared hard at Alex.

A second kid threw himself into the seat beside Calvin, took one look at Alex, and let out a creepy laugh. He laughed backwards, exhaling in a raspy pant and then making long, wheezy, squeaky yelps while he inhaled. This was Deemer. If he had a second name, nobody knew it. Deemer never said anything; he just wore a sick, pasted-on grin all the time like some kind of crazy clown.

But they didn't worry Alex.

The real trouble was coming down the aisle.

Jordan McCreevey.

Unlike Calvin and Deemer, who advertised their weirdness from a hundred yards away, Jordan kept his face so empty that the emptiness alone was menacing. With Calvin and Deemer, you knew what was coming. But Jordan's meanness could sneak up on you. That made him a hundred times more dangerous.

As Jordan made his way to the rear of the bus, kids shrank back in their seats, hoping to be passed over this day. He worked his way steadily down the aisle, never once looking at Alex. But somehow, Alex knew Jordan was coming for him. Alex forced himself to stare out the window, knowing not to make eye contact. He didn't have to look up to sense that Jordan was there. Armpit and Cheetos: he'd know that smell anywhere.

But to Alex's complete surprise, Jordan kept going, right past Alex's row.

Alex exhaled. He hadn't even realized he'd been holding his breath.

"Anyone sitting here?"

Jordan was right beside him.

Without waiting for an answer, Jordan started to flop down on the empty seat. Alex barely managed to snatch the box of cupcakes off the seat and onto his lap.

Jordan pointed at the bakery box.

"Birthday?" His voice was even, almost friendly.

Alex nodded. But he wasn't fooled. Jordan lifted up the corner of the box and peered inside.

"Bake 'em yourself?"

"My mom."

"My mom can't even cook toast."

He made this sound like it was Alex's fault.

Alex slid the cupcakes over to his right, away from Jordan, next to the bus wall.

"You better leave them alone."

Behind him, he heard Kwan gasp. No one told Jordan what to do.

Jordan looked right at Alex. "I'm not gonna touch 'em. Swear."

Alex clenched his jaw, smart enough not to lower his guard. Jordan turned back and continued to stare straight ahead with that same blank expression. They rode in silence, the hum of the bus the only noise. Up ahead, the road curved to the left. Mary Jo steered the bus into the turn.

As the centrifugal force pushed them sideways, Jordan slid across the seat and slammed hard into Alex, ramming him into the side of the bus and smashing the cupcakes into the wall. It happened so fast that Alex hadn't seen it coming.

Calvin and Deemer were laughing, beside themselves.

"Don't cry, crybaby," Deemer hissed.

Jordan continued to stare straight ahead, as if

nothing were going on.

As the bus came out of the turn, Jordan didn't let up. Alex could feel Jordan's hips flex as he pressed his feet into the floor, shoving his body harder and harder against Alex's, mashing him against the side of the bus. Alex tried to push back, but he had no leverage.

Pinned and powerless, with Jordan pressing into him with all his might, Alex found it hard to breathe. Even if he could have filled his lungs, he wouldn't have said a word to the bus driver. If he tried to get Jordan in trouble, Jordan would wiggle out of it, claiming it was an accident. That was Jordan's genius: he never got caught. Even now, as Mary Jo glanced back, all she saw above the seats was Jordan sitting quietly, staring calmly ahead.

And all Alex could do was sit there and take it.

He knew they couldn't be that far from school, but the rest of the ride seemed to take forever. Alex tried making deals with the universe, the way he usually did: "If I hold my breath to the count of thirty, he'll get bored and stop." "If I close my eyes for three more blocks, he'll let up."

Jordan never let up, even as he was telling dirty jokes to Calvin.

Deemer kept up a sing-song taunt: "Crybaby, crybaby, stick your head in pie, baby!"

Alex clamped his eyes closed, trying to shut

them out. He was in the middle of one of his deals, counting to forty-five this time, when the bus stopped hard for a red light. Alex opened his eyes, hoping to see their school out the window.

He saw something better.

A dog.

A muddy stray, nosing through a pile of trash next to an abandoned gas station. He wasn't much to look at, but the mere sight of him made Alex's heart lift.

Alex had imagined getting a dog for as long as he could remember. He'd thought up a hundred different names and pictured himself with every possible breed. Up to then, his dream of getting a dog had always seemed just that: a dream.

But as he stared at the stray, something lit up inside him. The dog had cornered a sock and was playing a game with himself, picking it up and flinging it across the ground, only to chase it down again. He was everything Alex had ever wished for, fun and feisty and full of mischief.

Alex knew with a certainty he couldn't explain that this dog was the one.

Then the dog looked up. Right at Alex.

They locked eyes. The dog stared at him, head cocked to one side. Alex stared right back.

"Hey, boy," Alex whispered.

The dog's ears twitched.

He heard me, Alex thought.

The light changed, and the bus started to move. Alex held the dog's gaze as the bus gained speed.

And then the dog took off in hot pursuit.

Alex twisted his neck around. "Go, boy," he whispered.

Miraculously, the dog started to gain on them. He was only half a block back, when suddenly the bus turned a corner, and the dog disappeared.

Alex's stomach dropped. He stared back, searching—

—and then the dog bolted out from an alley, right behind them. He'd found a shortcut! Alex couldn't believe how smart this dog was. The dog raced down the sidewalk after the bus. He was actually gaining on them.

And then the bus zoomed across a busy intersection. Four lanes each way. Sixteen lanes of traffic at rush hour.

A death zone.

"STAY!!!" Alex shouted.

Jordan turned toward him sharply.

Alex didn't notice. All he cared about was this: the dog stopped with one foot in the street, then pulled back onto the curb and sat down, staring after the bus.

"Good boy," Alex murmured under his breath, sad, but relieved.

He stared back until he couldn't see the dog anymore.

The bus finally pulled to a stop in front of Alex's school. The brakes hissed as Mary Jo turned off the engine and swung open the door.

Jordan stayed seated, still leaning into Alex, until the rows in front of them had emptied. At last, he eased off and yanked himself into the aisle. His eyes lingered over the crushed bakery box, cake and icing oozing out the seams. Then they flicked back to Alex.

"Happy birthday," he said.

CHAPTER 5
Worst. Birthday. Ever.

9:45 a.m.

Alex stared out the window of Room 15. He had spent all of homeroom and most of first period thinking about that dog. But then his stomach started to growl, and by second period he had a serious case of cupcakes-on-the-brain.

His teacher, Mrs. Hamlin, had given him a funny look when he handed her the cupcake box that morning. He had tried to reassure her that the cupcakes weren't a total loss. He figured he could scoop up the mashed remains like snowballs and mold them back into shape. Totally salvageable. "They're a little smashed, but they taste fine. I tested one to be sure." She looked at the box like she was considering throwing it away. But all she did was raise an eyebrow and set it on her desk.

Now Alex's stomach grew so noisy that Doug started growling back at it under his breath, which gave Kwan the giggles, which goaded Doug to growl even louder, which cracked up the rest of the class but also drew a look from Mrs. Hamlin. This was a problem, because Alex was trying to figure out how he could convince her to let them eat the cupcakes now.

Just as Alex was about to raise his hand and ask about the cupcakes, a runner came with a note for Mrs. Hamlin, who stepped out of the room to read it.

Alex sighed and lowered his hand. His mind drifted back to the stray dog. He couldn't explain it—after all, he'd only seen the dog for a few seconds—but when he thought about the dog, he felt the same way he'd felt when his dad put his hand on his shoulder at the air show, warm and happy and connected.

That dog had really gotten under his skin. Alex gazed out the window, half-expecting to see the yellow mutt waiting for him outside.

"Alex?"

He'd been daydreaming. Mrs. Hamlin stood at the front of the room, the note clutched in her hand.

"Pack up your bag, and let's go."

Alex looked around, confused. Chairs scraped as the other kids gathered up their backpacks and shuffled towards the door. The classroom was already half-empty.

"Alex, did you hear me? You're to pick up your sister from Room 4B and go straight to see your mother at work."

"Um, now?"

"Yes, now."

"We're leaving?"

"Yes. We're...finishing early today."

"But what about the box?"

"What box?"

"My cupcakes."

"Just leave it."

"But it's my bir—"

"Alex Douglas, not another word! We'll do it another day. Now let's go."

The one other time Alex could remember getting sent home early was when someone set off a stink bomb last year in the girls' bathroom. The smell was so gross that even the teachers were running outside, staggering around the playground and gasping for air. He heard six kids in the class next to the bathroom couldn't even make it to the trash can and puked all over their desks. School was canceled while they aired out the building that day, but it still smelled like rotten eggs for an entire week. The only person who seemed to think it was hilarious was Jordan.

Maybe Jordan was behind this, too. Alex sniffed the air but couldn't detect anything stink-bomby.

He looked over at Dougie and Kwan: what gives? They shrugged.

Mrs. Hamlin hurried them out the door. Her face looked bloodless, as gray as fireplace ash. When he tried to catch her eyes, she looked away.

He gave one last glance at the box of mangled cupcakes on her desk, then gave up and headed for the door. Next to the door hung the class calendar; he stared at the words written there in big green letters: "ALEX'S BIRTHDAY."

The date was even circled: September 11, 2001.

CHAPTER 6
The Man in the White Shirt

8:44 a.m.

Earlier that morning, across the river in lower Manhattan, a man in a white shirt made his way to the underground mall beneath the World Trade Center towers for coffee and a bagel, his usual morning pick-me-up.

Standing in line, he smiled to himself as he noticed all the other men dressed like him: white shirt, sleeves rolled up, dark pants, tie. The concourse was bustling with workers from the floors above who'd come down for a break, while new waves of commuters poured off the trains from the level below.

At 8:45 a.m., the Man in the White Shirt bit into his bagel and hit the button for the elevator. He checked his reflection in the elevator doors.

At 8:46, he felt the building shake.

People near him looked around anxiously.

"What was that?"

"You feel that?"

He walked back to the concourse to see what was going on. The place was buzzing. Storekeepers hovered nervously in doorways.

"What happened? What happened?"

And then it hit: a fireball exploded out of the elevator shaft, blowing the doors off the elevator where the Man in the White Shirt had just been standing.

Instantly, there was pandemonium as the concourse filled with inky black smoke.

A bank of lights flickered and went out. Sprinklers overhead came on, showering the crowds as they surged for the exits.

"Stay calm."

"FIRE! FIRE!"

"IT'S A BOMB!" someone shouted.

Then another rumor took hold and raced through the crowd like wildfire until it was repeated so often that it sounded like truth.

But the Man in the White Shirt couldn't believe it. He cut through the crowd and found a Port Authority police officer urging people to keep moving for the exits.

"What happened?" he asked.

"An airplane just hit the building."

CHAPTER 7
Sick

10:08 a.m.

"Mom?"

Alex startled his mother as he came up behind her at the hospital. She'd been on the phone, her back to the door, and she hadn't seen Alex and Nunu come in. She dropped the phone and ran around the counter to give them a hug. Behind her, a busy signal buzzed from the abandoned receiver.

Alex squirmed as the hug seemed to go on longer than normal.

"Take your sister over there and wait for me," his mom said quietly.

She pointed to the waiting area across from the

nurses' station.

"They canceled school," said Alex.

"I know."

"How come?"

"Just wait over there."

"But how come—"

"*Alex*. Please. Just take your sister over there and wait. I need a minute to think." His mother's voice sounded tight and thin, like a guitar string about to break.

Alex put a hand on Nunu's back and guided her to a bench in the waiting area, then pulled out his Gameboy. Nunu stared up at him.

"Alex?"

"Yep?"

"How come we're not in school?"

"I dunno."

"What are you playing?"

"A game."

"Can I see?"

He sighed but turned in his chair so she could watch. After losing four games in a row, he handed it over to let her play.

He couldn't keep his mind on the game anyway. He kept trying to figure out what was going on. First, they canceled school and sent everyone home. Then there was that strange bus ride over here; it was the quietest he'd ever heard a city bus.

Now his mom was acting all weird.

He snuck a glance at her. She was leaning against the counter with her back to him, the desk phone tucked under her chin. With her other hand, she dialed her cell phone, then fumbled the phone and nearly dropped it. Even from across the room, Alex could see her hand was shaking.

His mom turned and caught him staring. She forced a tiny, awkward smile, trying to reassure him, but Alex could tell something was up. He just couldn't tell what. Most of the time, his mom was calm and in charge and knew what to do. He'd seen her mad (usually at him), and he'd seen her impatient (usually with his dad), but he'd never seen her like this.

And it freaked him out a little.

Alex watched his mother snap the phone shut in frustration without reaching anyone. He wondered who she needed to call so badly.

His mom turned to her supervisor, a solid woman with a jaw like a bulldog's. They seemed to be having an argument. His mom kept gesturing towards the waiting room. Alex reached over and flipped the mute switch on the Gameboy. With the sound off, he could just catch bits and pieces of the conversation.

"What am I supposed to do?" his mother asked.

There was more back-and-forth that he missed.

Then he saw the bulldog shake her head. "I need you here. This could be a long night. Might get pretty ugly."

His mom glanced his way again. He twisted around and pretended to watch the Gameboy over Nunu's shoulder. A moment later, his mother appeared beside them.

"Alex, I need you to take your sister home and stay there until I get off work tonight."

Alex frowned. "Why?"

She hesitated, then took a deep breath and spoke carefully, as if she'd rehearsed what she was about to say.

"We've had an emergency, and they need me here all day. So I need you to take Nunu straight home and wait for me there. Can I count on you to do that?"

Of course he could do that. They rode the bus all the time, no problem.

"Who're you trying to call?" he asked, then made an educated guess. "Dad?"

"His line's busy. I'll get him later." She changed the subject. "You've got your cell phone?"

He nodded and pointed at his backpack.

"Baby, I'm sorry. I know it's your birthday—"

She tried to stroke his head, but he pulled away. "I'm not a baby."

"I know. I promise we'll have cake as soon as I

get home. Okay?"

Alex stared at his lap as questions filled his head. He wanted to know why she argued with her supervisor. And why they canceled school. And who she was calling and what the big emergency was and why his birthday was ruined.

"Alex." Something in her tone caught his attention. "Go straight home, and no TV. Play board games or read. Do you understand?"

She knelt in front of him. She looked as serious as he'd ever seen her look. When she spoke, her voice was quiet but clear.

"I need you to be a grown-up today."

CHAPTER 8
The Man in the White Shirt

9:01 a.m.

The Man in the White Shirt raced up the concourse stairs, searching for a way out of the smoke.

When he reached the ground floor, he emerged into a war zone. Burning debris littered the lobby. Smoke hung heavy in the air.

He ran for the exit, then stopped at the windows. The outdoor plaza was covered with twisted metal and shattered glass and broken furniture. Part of a desk crashed to the ground twenty yards away, on fire, as more and more flaming debris fell from above.

He turned back and headed for the other side of

the lobby just as a company of firefighters rushed in, nearly knocking him over. The firefighters charged upstairs, heavy hoses coiled over their shoulders. A nozzle from a hose caught the Man in the White Shirt on the elbow, and he jumped away, arm throbbing.

"Move it move it move it!" shouted a policeman, trying to herd people to safety.

The Man in the White Shirt kept moving.

When he reached the door, he could see pieces of wreckage lying around, but there wasn't as much debris falling on this side, not as much stuff on fire. He hoped nothing would land on him. He lowered his head and ran.

A block away, he slowed down and turned back to look.

There was a gaping hole in the side of the North Tower, ninety stories up. Red flames billowed out, surrounded by black smoke from the burning jet fuel.

The Man in the White Shirt thought of those people trapped on the upper floors, and of the firefighters who'd have to climb ninety flights to reach them. He hoped they'd get there in time.

"How could an accident like this happen?" he wondered. The skies were clear and bright; there wasn't a cloud in the sky. Didn't the pilot see where he was going?

Someone screamed nearby. He looked over, but they were pointing off to the west. A big commercial jet flew past, heading south. It seemed unusually low. It followed the Hudson River out toward the Statue of Liberty.

And then it banked.

It made a U-turn and headed back towards Manhattan.

It was flying straight at the World Trade Center.

The Man in the White Shirt watched in horror as it disappeared behind the buildings. Seconds later, he heard a loud impact as the plane hit the other side of the South Tower, sending an explosion of wreckage and flames straight through the building and out the north side.

He knew then that this was no accident.

CHAPTER 9
Be There

10:21 a.m.

Alex stared out the window of the city bus, hardly noticing the familiar landscape as a series of images rolled through his head: Jordan, wishing him happy birthday with a smirk; the crushed cupcakes he'd left behind; his dad's pants, the light catching on a faded crease; Mrs. Hamlin, her face as gray as ash; his mom, kneeling down to him, eye-to-eye.

Nothing made any sense today. And his birthday was officially ruined.

He caught a glimpse of himself in the window reflection. He looked like a pouty pre-schooler.

Yuck.

He looked away and tried to shake off his sulky mood. Then he noticed the strange silence on the bus. The other passengers all seemed to be staring at the floor. It was almost like his mood had infected the entire bus.

He heard a soft mumbling nearby. An old lady in the row behind him had her eyes closed while she counted her rosary, her lips moving silently as her trembling fingers pushed through the beads. A word of her prayer drifted to his ears.

"Father," she whispered.

Alex shivered. He checked out the window; they weren't even halfway home yet.

The light ahead turned red. The bus slowed to a stop.

He sat up a little straighter as he realized where they were: right next to the abandoned gas station where he saw the stray dog that morning. Behind a fence of jagged metal, the lot was covered in broken glass and rusty barrels. It was an ugly, dangerous place, and it made him feel bad to think of the dog all alone out here.

Then a new thought struck him: maybe that's why the dog ran after him this morning. Maybe the dog needed him just as much as he needed that dog.

He closed his eyes tightly and made a frantic

deal with the universe.

"If I close my eyes and count to ten," he whispered, "he'll be there."

He counted to ten, forcing himself to go slowly. Then he opened his eyes.

There was no sign of the dog anywhere.

Alex slumped. For a brief moment, he had believed, really believed. Now he just felt stupid.

Outside the bus, a dog barked.

Alex jerked up straight and looked out the window.

The stray dog sat outside, staring up at the bus like he'd been waiting there all morning. Waiting for Alex.

Alex locked eyes with the dog. The dog barked again.

Alex pointed at himself and asked, "Me?"

The dog nodded. Alex was a hundred thousand percent sure of it.

The light turned green. The bus pulled away from the intersection.

But half a block down, the bus made a noise like someone had punched it in the gut and knocked its wind out.

Phhhhhooooooossssshhhhhttttt.

The air brakes hissed as it jerked to a stop at the curb. The doors sprang open, and Alex popped out like a cork shot out of a bottle. He remembered to grab Nunu by the hand as he checked for traffic and sprinted back across the street.

"Alex? Where are we going?" Nunu panted, trying to keep up.

The dog watched them approach, his head cocked to one side.

"Alex?"

When he got ten feet away, Alex stopped. It was his first chance to see the dog up close. The mutt had an ice cream wrapper stuck to his back paw like a shoe; his other paws were covered in mud. There was a dark patch above his muzzle that made him look like he had a black eye. One of his ears stood straight up, while the other was turned inside out and flopped over backwards. And he was missing a bit of fur from his left haunch, where a patch of skin showed through, the same shade as the wad of bubble gum stuck to his tail. The dog shook his head, knocking the second ear back into place. His big pink tongue hung out of one side of his mouth, and as his head moved, it swung from side to side, flinging slobber.

He's the most beautiful dog ever, Alex thought.

Alex dropped to one knee and put his hand out.

"Hey there, boy."

The dog took one step forward.

Nunu knelt next to Alex, watching carefully.

The dog took another cautious step.

Then another.

Alex held perfectly still.

"That's a good boy. C'mon."

Alex didn't take his eyes off the dog.

"Alex?" Nunu whispered. "What're you doing?"

"Looks like I just found my birthday present," he said quietly. Nunu's eyes went huge.

The dog inched closer. He strained his neck forward to sniff at Alex's outstretched hand. Alex didn't move a muscle. The dog stuck his tongue out and tasted Alex's palm. It tickled. Alex held his breath as he slowly reached out to scratch the dog's ears.

The dog pounced, knocking him flat on his back. His heavy paws stood on Alex's shoulders, pinning him to the pavement. Alex started to panic.

Then the dog licked Alex up one side of his face and down the other with that gigantic pink tongue.

"Good boy! Down boy! Down boy!"

The dog leaned over and licked a kiss across Nunu's face, too, then stood back, his tail wagging like crazy. Nunu giggled as Alex burst out laughing. He rolled to his feet, and the dog let out a happy bark.

Dogs don't talk; Alex knew this. But at that moment, he could almost believe that this dog—his dog—was speaking to him.

He was wishing Alex a happy birthday.

CHAPTER 10
A Dog's Life

10:34 a.m.

Alex wanted to cram everything he'd ever thought of doing with a dog into that morning. He was sure his dog was thinking the same thing.

They were walking home, because Alex knew dogs weren't allowed on the bus. Half a block down, the dog found a stick and dropped it at Alex's feet. Alex gave it a gentle toss; the dog sprang up and caught it in mid-air as it left his hand.

Alex laughed. "So that's how you want to play it?"

The dog crouched, poised, as Alex turned toward an empty lot and hurled the stick as far as he could throw it. The dog took off at full speed. He didn't slow until the last second, paws skidding in the dirt, his butt sliding past as he lapped the stick up into his mouth. He raced back and proudly deposited the chewed-up prize at Alex's feet and then crouched, ready to go again.

As Alex watched his dog chase the stick again, a fleeting thought briefly darkened his mood, like a cloud passing over the sun. His parents hadn't gotten him a dog, so would they let them keep this one? But they'd have to, he thought. They'd have to! Once they met him and saw how great he was, there's no way they could say no.

When they reached a playground with nobody else around, Alex and Nunu and the dog jumped on the merry-go-round. But as soon as Alex started to spin them, the dog jumped off, barking in confusion. Alex and Nunu whirled themselves dizzy, then staggered off, teetering in wobbly circles until they both fell over laughing as the dog ran back and forth between them, like he wanted back in the game.

Then Alex took off his belt, held one end tight, and gave the other to the dog, who grabbed it in his mouth and took off running. Alex leaned back onto the wheels of his Heelys, and suddenly he was flying, arms outstretched, wind in his hair, laughing.

Alex had dreamed of dogs for as long as he

could remember. He had always known with absolute certainty that a dog would make everything better.

But he never knew it could be this good.

Having a dog more than made up for Jordan and the smashed cupcakes and the weird day. All the troubles of the morning just disappeared.

It was like all his deals with the universe had finally come true.

"Here, Max."

Alex called to the dog, who had stopped to sniff a light pole. The dog didn't respond but moved on to investigate a trash can.

Nunu looked at him funny. "Who's Max?"

"I'm trying out my top ten dog names. Does he look like a Max to you?"

Nunu shook her head. "Here, Muffin," she called.

Alex made a face. "Muffin?"

"It's better than Max."

"Dog names are like Rex. Or Charlie."

"Here, Buttons," Nunu tried again.

Alex rolled his eyes and called to the dog. "Here, Rex. C'mon, Charlie."

Nothing.

"Over here, Fang."

The dog ducked into some bushes.

Alex worked his way through the list: Buddy, Maverick, Genghis, Ralph, and Mugsy.

The dog didn't answer to a single one. Alex was down to his last pick.

"Here...Annihilator."

"That's not a doggy name!"

The dog chased his tail, spinning in circles, ignoring them completely.

"We should call him Twirly," Nunu observed.

"No." Alex's scowl only goaded Nunu on. She loved it when she could get under her big brother's skin.

"Or Poochy."

"No."

"Or Daisy."

"That's a girl name."

"How about Pee Pee?"

"Pee Pee??"

Nunu pointed: the dog had his leg up, leaving his mark on a mail box to alert the world that he'd been there.

"We're not calling him Pee Pee."

As they made their way through town, Alex still hadn't found the right name for his dog. But in every other respect, the universe was smiling on him today—especially when they saw what was sitting in the window of DiSarno's bakery. Right there in the main case, next to the trays of gingerbread men and fruit tarts and odd-looking foreign cookies, sat a platter piled four stories high.

With cupcakes.

Chocolate-frosted chocolate cupcakes. With chocolate fudge swirls on top.

"We're not supposed to have sweets before lunch," Nunu breathed, as the two of them stared in the window.

"Pick out the one you want," said Alex. "My treat."

The little bell over the door ding-a-linged as they stepped inside. The dog slipped in behind them. Alex tried to push him back out, but it was like trying to move a bus.

"Rex. C'mon. You gotta get out."

The dog just stood there, drooling, as he stared around at all the goodies.

"It's okay, Alex. There's nobody here."

The shop was empty. Even though the shades were up, the door was unlocked, and a neon sign buzzed "OPEN" in big red letters, there was nobody here. Alex jiggled the door to make the bell ring again. Still nobody.

He stepped cautiously behind the counter and peeked into the back. The baking tables were covered in flour. A big plastic tray full of glistening dough sat uncovered. An apron lay in a heap in the middle of the floor. Nearby, Alex could see a half-decorated cake with red letters on top that read *Happy b*. A piping bag lay on the table beside it, trailing a thread of red icing.

"Hello?"

No answer. It looked like everyone had left in a hurry.

"Weird." He turned back to the store. "There's nobod—HEY!"

The dog had his head buried in the display case and was licking an enormous white cake.

"Bad boy! Get out of there!"

Alex had to put both arms around the dog's neck and pull with all his might to get him out of the case. The dog's face was completely covered with white cake and icing. Then that enormous tongue poked out and spun clockwise around his face, squeegeeing the icing and cake away in one sloppy swipe.

Alex reached back into the case, lifted out two cupcakes, and handed one to his sister.

"One for you. And one for me."

"That's stealing," Nunu said. But she didn't give back her cupcake.

Alex dug into his pocket, pulled out his lunch money, and left three dollars on the counter.

While he was paying, the dog got back into the case and took a huge bite out of the white cake. Alex dug back into his pocket. He only had two dollars and forty-six cents left over, but he put it all on the counter, promising himself to stop by tomorrow and settle up.

Then something on the counter caught his eye: an open box of birthday candles.

He took out two green candles and poked them into the top of his cupcake, adjusting them so they stood side by side, straight and tall.

"There. Eleven."

He found a pack of matches tucked behind the cash register and lit the candles.

"Happy birthday to me."

Nunu joined in. When they got to *"Happy birthday to A - LEXXXX,"* the dog joined in too, howling all the way to the end.

"Happy birthday to MEEEEEEEEEE!"

"Make a wish," Nunu reminded him.

Alex already knew what to wish for. He knelt down even with the candles, so close he could feel their heat on his face. Then he made a silent wish, took a deep breath, and blew.

The flames flickered, pushed sideways by his breath, then went out, leaving two trails of smoke drifting slowly into the air.

CHAPTER 11
The Man in the White Shirt

9:59 a.m.

The Man in the White Shirt didn't see the first tower fall.

He felt it.

The ground rumbled and shook beneath his feet. Then the shockwave hit him, a metallic groan that quickly became a roar. He turned toward the sound and stared in utter disbelief as the South Tower began to collapse, all one hundred ten stories, crumpling down on itself in an explosion of glass and smoke and steel.

His feet were frozen to the pavement as he watched.

This can't be happening, he thought. There are people in there.

A chunk of glowing metal the size of a bus smashed down on the street in front of him. The shock of the impact blew out the store windows beside him and knocked him off his feet. He fell backwards and slammed his head on the pavement.

He didn't feel his cell phone shoot out of his shirt pocket, didn't hear it smash on the concrete and skitter in pieces into the gutter.

He pulled himself up and saw a woman lying in the street beside him. Her knees were bleeding, and she'd lost a shoe. He took her hand and pulled her to her feet. She stared past him in horror and then took off running. He looked back.

A dark gray cloud was rolling straight at him.

It roared up the street like a tsunami, a boiling swirl of dust and smoke blown out by the falling building. Ten stories high, then thirty, it blocked his view of whatever was behind it.

He turned to run. But the gray cloud overtook him.

CHAPTER 12
Home Run

10:49 a.m.

"What are you doing here?"

"What are YOU doing here? You never come outdoors."

"Mom said I had to," said Doug, who hated leaving his computer for anything but school or dinner.

Alex ran into Doug and Kwan in the park when Rex bolted into the trees to chase a squirrel. (Alex had decided to go with the name Rex and see if the dog would eventually answer to it. If that didn't work, he'd try a different name tomorrow.) This was perfect: he couldn't wait to show off his new dog.

If only he could find him.

Alex glanced around: some boys were hitting grounders with a tennis ball over on a nearby baseball diamond, but the rest of the park was empty; he couldn't spot Rex anywhere.

"My mom told me I couldn't sit in front of the TV all day," Doug grumbled.

Kwan nodded. "My mom said the same thing."

"Yeah. But this time, she actually unplugged it."

"My mom was acting all weird, too," Alex chimed in. He shook his head. "Parents."

Kwan and Doug nodded.

Alex heard a bark and spotted Rex rolling on his back in the outfield grass, wiggling and kicking his paws in the air. Nunu saw him, too, and giggled.

"Look at that dog," said Kwan. "What a doof."

"That's Rex. He's mine," Alex said proudly.

Kwan's eyebrows shot up. Doug's jaw fell open. Alex ate it up as his two friends stared at him in total disbelief.

"No way. Your parents actually got you a dog?" said Kwan.

Nunu started to correct them. "We found him on the road—"

"He's my birthday dog," Alex interrupted.

Shouting erupted from the baseball field. Alex turned to see Rex racing across the grass, chasing down a line drive tennis ball.

"NO BOY! STAY!"

Alex was off and running in an instant. Those kids on the ball field looked big, like they wouldn't appreciate having their ball stolen. The outfielder, a tall, squinty-eyed red-headed kid, chased after the ball. Alex turned on the afterburners. The dog, on the other hand, didn't even look like he was trying. He loped across the grass, easily outraced them all, and gobbled the ball up, sweeping it into his jaws with that huge tongue. He turned without missing a beat, sprinted straight back, and dropped his prize catch at Alex's feet, where it landed with a soggy plop.

Alex picked up the ball just as the redheaded outfielder came running up. He was even bigger up close—at least a seventh grader.

Alex held out the wet ball. "Sorry," he murmured.

The redheaded boy squinted at the ball, then took it back. The dog stared at the ball with laser-like focus, hoping for another round of fetch. The redheaded boy watched him watch the ball, then broke into a smile. "No sweat. He made a good catch."

Alex grinned with relief and scratched Rex behind the ears.

"Hey, you guys wanna play?"

"Really?" Alex glanced at Doug and Kwan.

"Three more, and we'd have five a side."

"I'm in!" Dougie shouted. Alex threw him a funny look as he ran past. "This is the first time I've ever been picked for baseball. Let's go before he changes his mind."

It wasn't the greatest game ever. But no one ever had more fun with a skinny bat and a tennis ball covered in dog goober.

Kwan got three hits, scored one run, and made two put-outs.

Doug dropped two fly balls, struck out twice, got hit in the chest by a line drive, and let five grounders go between his legs. But he never once stopped smiling.

Nunu watched from the dugout, sitting on Alex's backpack so she could see the field. Rex stretched out next to her, his big head in her lap.

Alex never had a single strike; every swing of the bat connected. He hit a triple, a ground-out, and two doubles. In the bottom of the ninth, he connected on a long line drive that was still rising as it flew over the center fielder's head.

"Yes!" Alex pumped his fist and started jogging around the bases. No way the outfielder could get to it in time. It was a sure home run. He was playing skins and had his shirt tied around his head; as he ran, the sleeves swung like elephant trunks.

Then he saw Rex go tearing after the ball.

"No!" cried Alex.

"Yes!" cried the other team.

Rex got to the ball, hoovered it up, and started back towards Alex. Alex saw him coming and broke into a sprint. The dog seemed to think this was part of the game and turned on the juice. As Alex rounded second base, Rex passed the center fielder and was closing fast.

"C'MON! BRING IT HOME!" cheered the other team as they frantically waved the dog in.

"HE'S AT SECOND! MOVE IT!!" Alex's teammates shouted.

Alex hit third base and rounded the corner without breaking stride. Rex headed straight across the infield; to him, it was just a game of fetch, but to the players it looked exactly like he was trying to beat the runner and make the tag at home plate.

Alex lowered his head and pumped his arms.

Rex leaped the pitcher's mound in one stride.

It was going to be close.

Out of the corner of his eye, Alex saw a yellow-brown blur racing in. Alex tucked his knee and slid for home, throwing up a huge cloud of dirt.

Then they both vanished inside the swirling dust.

CHAPTER 13
The Man in the White Shirt

10:02 a.m.

The Man in the White Shirt staggered through the choking gray cloud. He couldn't see where he was going. He couldn't see anything.

He nearly crashed into a light pole that appeared a foot in front of him.

He heard others around him, panting as they ran.

Someone slammed into him from behind and then disappeared into the cloud.

He spun around, disoriented. His eyes stung. He was surrounded by smoke. He couldn't see five feet ahead. He had no idea which way to run.

He picked a direction and started forward, then bounced off something large and rubbery. He stepped back and realized what it was: a huge tire attached to an airplane's landing gear. It had broken off one of the planes and shot through the tower to land all the way out here in the street.

He heard more people running past and followed the sound of their feet.

The Man in the White Shirt ran until the air around him grew brighter. The cloud began to thin. He sprinted for the light, and then he was free, back in the sunshine.

Two fire engines raced past him, sirens blaring. A policeman on the next corner guided the trucks through the crowd, then continued directing the refugees uptown, away from the disaster, to safety.

The Man in the White Shirt stopped to catch his breath. Coughing, chest heaving, he looked back at the devastation he'd just escaped: one tower continued to burn; smoke and flames still roared from the upper floors.

But where its twin once stood, now there was a hole in the sky.

CHAPTER 14
Terror

11:12 a.m.

"Safe!"

Alex casually knocked the dust off his pants, just like the pros did on TV. He didn't really beat the tag; Rex had just dropped the ball at his feet. Still, a home run's a home run. He glanced at the dugout to see if Nunu had witnessed his triumph, so she could vouch for his story at dinner; but she'd found his Gameboy and wasn't paying him any attention. His teammates, though, treated him like a hero. As the game broke up, they pounded him on the back.

"Your dog rocks," said Kwan, patting Rex on the head.

"Guys?" Doug suddenly looked worried. "Don't tell my mom I had fun, okay? I don't want her making this no-TV thing a habit."

Alex's cell phone started to ring. He dug it out of his pocket and checked the number: his mom. Uh-oh.

"Mom. Hi. What's up?"

"I'm just checking in, wanted to make sure you guys are okay."

"We're fine."

"No problems on the bus?"

"Nuh-unh."

"What are you doing?"

"Nothing."

"What's all that noise in the background?"

"I'm, uh, messing around with Dougie and Kwan." Alex held up the phone. "Say hi, guys."

"Hi, Mrs. Douglas."

"Where's your sister?"

"Playing with the Gameboy."

"You didn't turn on the TV did you? Remember what I told you—"

"Mom—"

"Alex, you promised me."

"I know. We haven't watched TV. Promise."

There was silence on the line.

"When are you coming home?" he asked.

"I don't know yet. We might get busy."

He silently pumped his fist. That meant he still had hours to go before he had to explain about the dog.

"I'll call you later," she said.

"Okay."

"TV off, okay?"

"It IS off."

"And it stays off."

"O-*kay*." He waited, hoping she was done. "Is that it?"

"I guess so. I love you, hon."

Alex winced and looked at the guys. No way he could answer her back. "Uh, yeah, 'kay. Bye, Mom."

As he hung up, Dougie grinned at him. "Nice. You totally lied to your mother about being home."

"I didn't lie. I just didn't tell her the whole truth."

"Mayday Mayday Mayday," Kwan urgently cut in. "Bogeys at two o'clock."

Alex looked around. Jordan McCreevey was standing directly behind him, with Calvin and Deemer backing him up.

"Would you look at this? The Three Musketeers: a geek, a freak, and a crybaby."

Alex heard shoes slapping pavement. Kwan and Doug were running away.

"A-Dawg! C'mon!" shouted Kwan.

But Alex stood his ground.

Jordan snickered. "Did he just call you a dog?"

"A-Dawg. It's my call sign on Screaming Eagles IV."

Calvin leaned forward, impressed. "You've got Screaming Eagles IV?"

Jordan turned his head slightly towards Calvin, who instantly knew he'd screwed up for speaking without permission. Calvin dropped his eyes to the ground, then folded his arms and glared at Alex like it was *his* fault.

Jordan jerked his chin at the shirt still tied around Alex's head.

"What're you supposed to be, some kind of raghead?"

"I bet he's one of them," Deemer said.

"One of who?" asked Alex.

Deemer gave a crazy hoot. "You don't know?"

'They don't tell crybabies," Jordan explained.

Alex felt his face go red. "I'm not a crybaby," he said through gritted teeth. "But you're a jerk."

Calvin's eyes got wide. Deemer blinked in surprise. Jordan took a step towards Alex.

"And my dog thinks so, too," Alex added.

Jordan stopped. "What dog?"

Alex reached back to put a hand on Rex's head. And touched nothing.

He turned. No dog.

Alex took off like a fighter jet launched off an

aircraft carrier. Halfway across the park, he glanced over his shoulder. Calvin was huffing and puffing and drenched in sweat as he struggled to haul his bulk after Alex. Deemer looked like his limbs were made of springs that sent him lurching ahead in a series of herky-jerky leaps and bounds.

But Jordan, tall and lean and long-legged, was closing fast.

Alex knew he couldn't outrun them for long. He veered across an asphalt playground, vaulted over a seesaw, and dodged through a swing set. Out of the corner of his eye, he saw Deemer angling to cut him off.

Up ahead, the playground came to an abrupt end at a railing overlooking a steep drop, where a long stairway led to a lower level of the park. He veered left, straight across Deemer's path. Deemer saw him coming and closed the gap between them in three long strides. His hand brushed the tails of Alex's shirt. But Alex felt a burst of adrenaline and sprang free, jumping onto the stairway rail and grinding down the pipe on his Heelys, leaving Deemer swinging at empty air.

Alex landed perfectly on the path at the bottom, dropped into a tuck, and zoomed down the asphalt. When he'd put some distance behind him, he angled toward a brick restroom building, hoping to duck behind it and hide. As he whipped around the corner of the building, he took one last glance behind: Calvin was yelling at Deemer. They weren't watching him at all. Alex breathed a sigh of relief.

The hand caught him on the throat like a clothesline.

But his feet kept going. They shot out from under him as the hand tightened its grip and pulled him upright, until he was staring into the cold, blank eyes of Jordan McCreevey.

Alex tried to form a word. Nothing came out. He could feel the blood thudding in his head.

And then Jordan dropped him like a bag of trash. Alex landed on his knees, gasping for air. He staggered to his feet and noticed they weren't alone anymore: Calvin and Deemer had arrived.

Jordan nodded at the goons. Alex was still trying to regain his balance when they grabbed him from behind and yanked his arms back hard. He heard his shoulder pop and saw a flash of white as pain shot through his head like lightning.

Jordan stood in front of him. Only his hand moved down by his side; his fingers flexed, then tightened. He drew his arm back and cocked his fist like a hammer.

That's when the dog growled.

Jordan froze. He turned his head slowly, just enough to see Rex crouching behind him, back straight, ears swept forward, tail rigid and taut.

"Scat. Go away." Jordan muttered.

The dog's ears twitched. He drew back his lips and growled again.

"Stay," said Alex. "Good boy."

"He's yours?"

Alex nodded. Rex growled at Calvin and Deemer. They let go of Alex and stepped back. The dog took a step forward.

Jordan flinched. "Call him off."

"I don't think I can. He's wild."

Jordan snarled at his goons. "What're you mouth breathers staring at? Get over here!"

They didn't move a muscle.

Rex took another step. Jordan backed into the brick wall. His eyes darted left and right, looking for a way out.

"Call him off." Jordan jabbed his finger at Alex as he said it.

The dog read it as a threat and lunged at Jordan. Jordan turned and ran. He blew past a startled Calvin and Deemer, who fled right behind him. Rex paid them no attention; he bounded past like they were standing still and quickly closed the gap on Jordan, nipping at his heels and chasing him out of the park and down the block.

Alex followed them to the edge of the park. He cupped his hands around his mouth and shouted.

"HERE, BOY!"

Rex immediately stopped running. He stared after Jordan until he was certain that the bully wasn't coming back. Then he turned around and came loping back to Alex.

Alex knelt down as his dog sprinted the last few feet and jumped into his arms. Alex hugged him tight, but Rex squirmed and wriggled free, took a step back, and dropped something at Alex's feet.

Alex saw it and grinned.

It was a back pocket, torn from a pair of jeans.

"You are the coolest dog in the world."

He bent down to scratch Rex's ears, but the dog jumped up and down, licking Alex on the face as Alex rough-housed with him, celebrating their daring escape. Rex was in mid-jump when Alex suddenly stopped in his tracks. The dog landed on all fours and held still, head tilted to one side, alert to the abrupt change in Alex's mood.

Alex frowned and stared back across the empty park.

"Where's Nunu?

CHAPTER 15
Missing

11:22 a.m.

Alex sprinted up the concrete stairs to the upper playground.

"Be there be there be there," he whispered, taking the steps two at a time. He'd already made a hurried deal with the universe: if he took the steps two at a time, she'd be there.

When he reached the top, the playground was empty. There was nobody in sight.

There was no sign of Nunu anywhere.

He called out tentatively. "Nunu?"

He tried again, louder. "NUNU!!"

He shaded his eyes and scanned the park. Down

at the ball field, something in the dugout caught his attention. He sprinted over: it was his backpack, lying on the bench.

But no Nunu.

Alex turned in a circle, confused. This doesn't make any sense, he thought. Nunu never left his side; most of the time, he couldn't get rid of her. How could she just disappear?

Alex felt panic well up inside him as his brain jumped right to the worst-case scenario: Stranger Danger. They'd been taught it a thousand times in school. "Stranger Danger," their parents recited, over and over. So she had to know not to talk to strangers. But his parents had also taught Alex to watch after his sister when they were out together. If he could forget, so could she.

He tried to think back to when he'd last noticed her. It was at the end of the ballgame, when she was playing with the Gameboy. He hadn't seen her since then.

Alex swallowed hard to keep from being sick.

He felt a nudge on his leg and looked down: the dog had brought him a stick.

"No. We have to find Nunu."

Alex pushed on, searching the bathrooms and double-checking the playground. He ran across the huge, grassy expanse of the soccer field. Rex loped around him and kept bringing him sticks, looking hurt when Alex ignored him.

Alex turned back to the park and cupped his hands to his mouth. "NUNUUUU!!"

Rex tipped his head back and unleashed a long, serious howl.

"Shhh! Be quiet so I can hear!"

But every time Alex yelled, the dog howled right along with him.

They made their way around the edge of the park. Alex kept his eyes peeled.

"C'mon, Rex! Look for Nunu!"

The dog didn't seem to understand. He just kept getting tangled in Alex's legs and then veering off to sniff around benches and dig inside trash barrels.

Alex forged his way along a wild and overgrown creek bed, criss-crossing the muddy banks of the stream until it abruptly disappeared through a metal grate into a slime-slick culvert running under a four-lane road that bridged the far edge of the park. Alex tried the grate: it was welded shut. He peered inside but couldn't see anything.

Next to the culvert, a dusty maintenance yard ran all the way back into the shadows under the four-lane bridge. On the left, huge concrete pipes from an older sewer repair job lay scattered around. Over to the right stood an old shed, the door hanging slightly open.

Alex squeezed through a hole in the fence and

hurried toward the shed.

"Please be there. Please be there."

He reached the door and yanked it open.

The shed was empty.

Up to now, Alex had been able to hold it together. Now his knees started to shake. Tears burned his eyes.

Behind him, Rex began barking furiously.

Alex backed out of the shed. The dog was on the other side of the maintenance yard with his head inside a four-foot-wide concrete pipe, tail rigid, back feet bouncing nervously. Alex sprinted over and shoved his head in beside the dog's.

Nunu took one hand off the Gameboy controls and waved. "Hi, Alex."

Alex grabbed her by the hand and dragged her sideways out of the pipe.

"WHAT ARE YOU DOING IN THERE??"

"Playing Dora."

"YOU RAN AWAY!"

"I couldn't see the screen in the sun."

"I'VE BEEN LOOKING EVERYWHERE FOR YOU!"

"Why are you yelling at me??"

"I'M NOT YELLING!"

Once again, Rex howled right along with Alex.

When Alex and Nunu saw what was happening, they both got the giggles and couldn't stop. Rex stopped howling and let loose a happy bark.

"Sorry I yelled at you," said Alex.

"S'okay."

"I was worried."

"Not me."

Alex rolled his eyes, then grinned at his dog, who was scratching intently behind one ear, like nothing had happened. "You're lucky I've got the greatest rescue dog ever."

"HEY, CRYBABY!"

Alex spun around. Jordan and his goons were up on the bridge. Calvin seemed to be arguing with Jordan, but Jordan shoved him aside, then whipped his arm forward.

The beer bottle was in mid-air before Alex realized Jordan had thrown it.

"NO!"

The bottle hit with a sickening thud, followed by the sound of shattering glass.

The dog yelped once, and then his front legs buckled.

CHAPTER 16
The Man in the White Shirt

10:24 a.m.

The Man in the White Shirt turned a corner and saw a female police officer helping an injured man in a suit limp down the street. The police officer had lost her hat; her pants leg was dusty and torn. The businessman was in worse shape: he had no shoes; one foot was covered in blood; he couldn't put pressure on his ankle and held onto the cop's shoulder like a crutch.

The Man in the White Shirt angled towards them. He started to speak. At first, all that came out was a hoarse croak, and then he was choking, coughing, hacking the gritty gray dust out of his throat and lungs. The cop looked impatient; the last thing she needed was another invalid on her hands.

Finally, the coughing stopped, and he croaked out a question.

"Can I help?"

The cop threw him a look. "You up for it?"

The Man in the White Shirt nodded and got on the other side. He and the cop linked hands and made a cradle. The injured man put his arms around their shoulders and lowered himself into the basket they had made with their arms. Then they lifted him off his feet and carried him down the street, three people moving as one.

CHAPTER 17
Radar

11:34 a.m.

Alex's arms were on fire. But he barely noticed. Even though the dog was nearly half his size, Alex carried him the entire way, moving so fast that Nunu sometimes had to run to keep up. The dog laid his head on Alex's shoulder, blood seeping from behind his ear and matting his fur.

Alex whispered to him reassuringly. "It's okay, boy. You'll be okay."

Alex had passed the Happy Dog Animal Hospital a zillion times on the school bus. It was a low, white building painted with Dalmatian spots and a rotating sign out front shaped like a dog bone. Alex long ago made up his mind that when he got a dog, this would be his vet.

"I'm sorry, boy. I'm so sorry."

"Is he okay? Alex?" Nunu trotted anxiously behind them, holding onto the dog's paw and cooing, "Good boy."

"Alex, is he gonna be okay?"

"I don't know," said Alex.

"Who did it?"

"Some jerks."

"Why did they hurt him?"

"Because."

"Because why?"

"Because they're jerks."

"But why?"

"*I don't know,*" Alex replied sharply. "They just are."

They arrived at the vet's door just as the vet was locking up to leave. But the vet took one look at the injured dog, gave them a reassuring smile, and led them inside.

Dr. Marks was quick but thorough and soon reassured Alex that Rex was going to be fine. The dog just needed some stitches to close up the cut on his head. Alex stayed right by Rex's side through the whole exam, holding him while the vet irrigated the wound and stroking his paw when the doctor injected the cut with anesthetic. And when the doctor sewed the two flaps of skin together with needle and thread, Alex flinched but never looked away.

"There. Good as new. Just rub this cream on the wound twice a day." Dr. Marks held out a tube of ointment.

"I can't."

"It's not hard. I'll show you."

"No, I mean, I don't have any money."

Dr. Marks slapped the tube into Alex's hand. "This one's on the house," he said as he scratched the dog's neck.

"What's his name?"

"Um, well...see...the thing is...."

"You don't know your own dog's name?"

Alex hesitated. "I found him today. He's mine. He's my birthday dog. I'm gonna call him Rex."

The vet took a hand-held electronic scanner off the counter and waved it back and forth over the dog's back. The scanner beeped.

"He's got a chip."

The vet checked the read-out and nodded.

"Say hello to Radar."

"Radar," Alex echoed.

Radar turned at the sound of his name and licked Alex's hand.

"He's got an address, too."

The vet copied an address onto a pad, tore off the sheet, and held it out to Alex. "417 Van Orton.

You know where it is?"

Alex shrugged.

"That's his home. You should take him back," the doctor said.

Alex felt hot and cold all at once and reached for Radar to steady himself.

"No way. He's mine."

"He belongs to someone else." Dr. Marks's voice was quiet but firm.

"I found him."

The vet took off his glasses and rubbed the bridge of his nose. "Look, son, I don't have time to deal with this now. I've got to close up and get home to my family."

"He's mine."

"Where are your parents?"

Alex did not want his parents getting wind of any of this. "Okay, fine, give me the address. I'll take him back." He came around the table and reached for the paper.

The vet pulled it away. "Where are your parents?"

"My mom's in the hospital."

"Oh. Is she okay?"

"I guess. She's a nurse."

"Ah. What about your dad?"

"He's under the river."

"What?"

"That's what he always says. He drives the PATH train under the river to the World Trade Center."

"Oh, lord."

"What?"

"You don't know?"

That was the second time today he'd been asked that.

"Yeah," said Alex. Then he shrugged. "I think."

Dr. Marks glanced out at Nunu in the waiting room. He lowered his voice, turned back to Alex, and put a hand on his shoulder.

"Son, a bunch of terrorists just flew two planes into the World Trade Center."

CHAPTER 18
Questions

12:00 noon

Now Alex knew.

That's what Jordan and his goons were talking about when they asked, "You don't know?" That's why everyone got sent home early from school. That's why the people on the bus looked worried, and why his mother was stuck at work, and why he was supposed to bring Nunu straight home, and why all his friends had been told to leave the TV off. All those weird moments that had been bugging him since second period suddenly made sense. It was like a Rubik's cube, where everything seems like a total jumble until all the pieces slide into place at once.

For a split-second, he understood.

Then a flood of new questions filled his head. Who did it? Why did they do it? How could those huge towers just collapse? Did anyone die? How many? Now that he knew, he wanted to know more.

He thought of his father, driving a train straight to the World Trade Center.

A new question shoved all the others aside.

Would his dad be coming home?

CHAPTER 19
Mac

12:00 noon

Across town, in a little house that looked a lot like Alex's, an old man sat in his den, watching the disaster unfold on TV. Like Alex—like people all over the world that day—his head was full of questions. He was desperate for news and searching for answers.

His name was MacKnight. Everyone called him Mac.

His grown son, Bobby, called him Pop.

Mac's wife—Bobby's mother—was a retired schoolteacher named Dottie. After she stopped teaching, Dottie had kept herself busy volunteering at the library, until Alzheimer's clouded her brain and left her unable to take care of herself. Now she sat by the television all day, smiling sweetly and watching SpongeBob.

When Dottie first grew ill, Mac had struggled to provide the care she needed. Mac didn't complain, but Bobby knew it was hard on his dad; his father would never admit it, but he was lonely. So even though Bobby was in his mid-thirties, he gave up his Manhattan apartment and moved back home. He told his dad it was to help take care of his mom, but the truth is that Mac needed Bobby just as much as Dottie did.

Now every morning, Mac would rise early to put on a pot of coffee, and Bobby would come down in his clean white shirt, his tie loosened and sleeves unbuttoned.

"Good morning, Pop," he'd say.

"What's so good about it?" Mac would grumble.

It was their little joke, part of their morning routine. Then father and son would quietly read the paper and sip their coffee together before Bobby would rise, pat his Pop on the shoulder, and head off to ride the commuter train into Manhattan.

Bobby worked in the World Trade Center.

Now a single question ran through Mac's head, over and over: would his son be coming home?

CHAPTER 20
The Man in the White Shirt

12:00 noon

The Man in the White Shirt helped the cop lower another injured victim onto a plastic chair. They were inside a makeshift medical tent that had been set up just beyond the disaster zone. He and the cop had somehow become a team; this was the fifth person they'd carried over from West Broadway. The injured man tried to thank them, but a nurse told them to move so she could take the man's vital signs and check his wounds.

The Man in the White Shirt stepped back to let her do her job. A voice on the cop's radio cut through the static. The cop paused to listen, then ran back to the street and disappeared around a corner, headed south. She was gone before the Man in the White Shirt could say goodbye. Only then did he realize he didn't even know the cop's name.

The Man in the White Shirt stepped outside. Suddenly, he felt very, very alone. His hands began to tremble, and his legs started to quiver. He sat down heavily on the curb. At first, he thought that it was muscle fatigue from carrying all those injured people. He just needed a moment to rest.

Then his eyes started to burn. He blinked, and a warm tear rolled down his cheek.

What he needed wasn't rest. He needed his family. He needed to go home.

CHAPTER 21
Crossing the Bridge

12:15 p.m.

"Alex? Where are we going?"

Alex wasn't sure. His feet seemed to have a mind of their own.

Nunu held Alex tightly by the hand as he marched on, jaw clenched. He was carrying her backpack now, wearing it across his chest and his own on his back, but she still had to walk fast to keep up. Radar trotted along on his other side, bandaged but none the worse for wear.

"Alex?" Nunu tugged at his hand.

Alex stopped walking, staring in surprise as he saw where his feet had brought him. They were coming up to the bridge, the tall one they crossed on the bus ride to school every morning.

The one that let him see all the way to Manhattan.

Up ahead, policemen on horses clip-clopped across the bridge, eyeing every car that passed, checking the terrain below. Two more police cars drove slowly by; they paused briefly for the officers to exchange a few words with the men on horseback, then moved on.

Before he'd gone to the vet's office, Alex hadn't noticed the heavy police presence on the streets. Now he saw them all over town. Like they were on high alert or something.

"Alex?" Nunu sounded impatient. "You said we'd go home after."

Alex waited for the police to move on. He was afraid they might not let kids on the bridge. He realized why he was here. He had to see for himself.

When the police were out of sight, he set the backpacks down beside Nunu.

"Wait here. Don't move. You too, Radar. Stay."

Radar sat down obediently. Nunu looked frustrated but leaned on the guardrail next to Radar.

Alex kept his eyes down as he made his way to the center of the bridge, the highest spot. Then he slowly lifted his head to face Manhattan.

The Twin Towers were gone.

Where they once stood, a huge cloud of smoke and dust billowed up from the ground and trailed off to the east.

Alex stared. It didn't seem possible. He held up two fingers where the towers should be, trying to fix the view, trying to make it right.

He felt dizzy and gripped the railing tightly. Somewhere under that smoke was his dad. He remembered the last time he'd seen his father: last night, in the dark, at the bedroom door.

"I hate you," Alex had said.

Alex heard the words in his head and shivered. His father was in trouble, and Alex knew why.

He'd said the ugliest thing possible to his dad, and now he was paying the price.

The universe was evening the score.

"This is all my fault," he whispered.

Alex continued to stare at the broken skyline. His mind raced as he struggled to think of a way out of this. He had to undo the damage and bring his father home.

"What do I do?"

Radar whimpered and licked his hand. The dog had come to his side, like the answer to a question. Alex stared down at his new best friend.

And then a deal began to take shape in his head. He ran it forwards and backwards. The more he thought about it, the more certain he became. He was going to have to give up something big—big enough to make up for what he'd done.

Big enough to bring his father home.

He was going to have to make a tremendous sacrifice.

He was going to have to give up Radar.

CHAPTER 22
New Deal

12:15 p.m.

Mac closed his eyes and made another deal: if he stopped watching the news, the phone would ring.

He'd been sitting there all morning, glued to the TV. Now he turned away from the disturbing news reports and forced himself to stare at the phone, trying to make it ring.

The phone didn't ring.

He was on the sofa in the den, in his usual spot on the right-hand end. Bobby always sat on the left. Most nights, after Dottie was in bed, Bobby would join Mac there on the sofa to watch the nightly news. It felt wrong to Mac to be sitting here without Bobby by his side.

He continued to stare at the phone.

The phone didn't ring.

Maybe I need to shake things up, he thought. He got up and walked around the house. He turned off the coffee pot. He looked in on Dottie. He walked out to the porch, glanced up and down the empty street, came inside, and wound up right back where he started, on the couch.

As he settled into his usual spot, he glanced over at Bobby's side of the sofa. They'd sat there so many nights that the empty sofa cushions still held the shape of their bodies like a memory. Mac slid over, into Bobby's spot. He enjoyed the strangeness of sitting in the wrong seat, and then feeling his son's presence as the cushion molded around him and held him close.

He could see the phone out of the corner of his eye but forced himself not to look. This was his new deal: if he didn't look, the phone would ring.

He imagined the call he felt sure would come soon. The phone would ring, he'd answer, and then he'd hear two words: "Hi, Pop."

The thought made him smile. It wouldn't be long now.

CHAPTER 23
Whirlwind

12:23 p.m.

"Where are we going?" Nunu struggled to keep up as Alex led them through town.

"We're taking Radar home."

"Our home?"

"His home," Alex replied through clenched teeth.

"Why?"

Alex groaned inside. The Why game again.

"Because I have to."

"But you just got him."

"I know."

"Don't you want to keep him?"

"Duh."

"Then why?"

He knew if he tried to say it out loud, it wouldn't make any sense. Besides, how could he tell anyone the truth, that all of this was his fault?

"I have to."

"But why?"

"I just have to! Okay?"

Nunu frowned. Her brother wasn't making any sense.

Alex glared at her, wishing she'd just be quiet and leave him alone. The more questions she asked, the worse he felt, and if she asked one more question, he just might tell her everything.

A blizzard of papers whirled around Alex and Nunu. Radar was furiously swinging Alex's backpack in his mouth, shaking it like a rag doll, spilling notebook paper and sheets of homework everywhere. Alex made no move to stop him, not when they had so little time left together. He just watched as the whirlwind of paper swirled around their heads.

CHAPTER 24
The Man in the White Shirt

12:23 p.m.

The Man in the White Shirt found himself in a blizzard of memos and printouts, business cards and stationery, paper towels and copy paper, swirling through the air.

Blowing up the street from the south, where the towers once stood.

Strangely, it reminded him of a ticker-tape parade he'd gone to a few years ago, when the Yankees won the World Series. He'd taken off work, made it a father-son outing. He smiled at the memory; it was one of their best days together.

The sound of breaking glass cut into his

thoughts. He'd stepped on a picture frame: someone's family photo. A father and son. How had it landed here, so many blocks away? Did someone drop it while running? Or had it been hurled all this distance? He lifted the photo and leaned it against a building, where someone could find it if they came looking. He knew it was pointless, but he just couldn't leave the family behind on the pavement.

As he straightened up, he caught a glimpse of himself in a store window: a gray ghost stared back. When he left home this morning, he was wearing a white shirt and dark pants and shoes. Now, he was coated top to bottom with ash and soot; his hair, his face—even his eyelashes were coated in a fine gray powder.

He slapped at his pants, trying to knock out the dust. He noticed that even though the pants were now the color of old snow, somehow, the crease held its line. And where the fabric was creased, no dust clung to it. He couldn't stop staring at that razor-sharp line. It seemed so out of place, a reminder of how normal and ordinary his life had been when he left home this morning.

CHAPTER 25
Ghosts

12:46 p.m.

"Who are you calling?"

"Mom."

Alex flipped his phone shut, then opened it and tried again, willing the call to go through. His eyes landed on a billboard atop an apartment building. It showed an airplane flying over the rooftops, and a cheap fare to Boston, under the slogan, "We Bring the World to You." He'd probably seen it a thousand times before. Today, it made him shudder.

He put a finger in his other ear, listening hard. But once again, the phone beeped twice, then went dead. He checked the screen, though he already knew the message he would see: "CALL FAILED."

Nunu tugged at his shirt. "Alex."

"What?" She pointed down the street.

Alex thought he was seeing a ghost.

Then another. And another.

They were walking uphill from the dock, some moving slowly and painfully, all of them pale and gray.

"Who are they?" Nunu asked in a shaky whisper.

Alex shook his head and drew back, sheltering Nunu behind his leg, trying not to let her see he was scared. Only when the ghostly figures got closer did Alex realize these were just regular people, their clothes and hair and faces coated in gray dust and ash. Why? Why were they so dirty? he wondered. Behind them came dozens more, traipsing off the dock. Off the ferry boat from Manhattan.

Finally, it hit him. He waited until one of them passed close by, a man with only one shoe, walking gingerly on the ball of his bare foot.

"Were you at the World Trade Center?" Alex asked.

The man nodded. "We were lucky," he said hoarsely, then continued on.

These were the survivors, Alex realized, making their way home.

Until that moment, as horrible as the disaster had sounded to Alex, it had still felt far away and distant, across the river. Even when he'd seen the smoke from the fallen towers, it hadn't quite seemed possible. A part of him just couldn't believe it was real.

Now it was right in front of him, close enough to touch. A real live person who'd been there, in the middle of the disaster.

A real person, just like his father.

"Who was that?" asked Nunu.

Alex glanced down at his sister. Her constant barrage of questions usually annoyed him. She could be such a pest. Now, she just looked small and afraid.

"They look like ghosts," she whispered.

What should he tell her? He looked at the refugees, then back to Nunu.

"No." She was watching him intently, hanging on his words. "No, those aren't ghosts." He fumbled for more but came up blank. Then he spotted a Dunkin' Donuts ad on a bus bench. The ad pictured a cup of orange juice and a piping hot blueberry muffin.

"Those are...the Muffin People."

Nunu's eyes got a little bigger. "The what?"

"You don't know about the Muffin People?" He was totally winging it here.

Nunu shook her head.

"They were trying to make the, um, the biggest

blueberry muffin in the world. So they could get in the Guinness Book of World Records and be all rich and famous and stuff."

"How big?"

"Big. I think they used, like, uh, four million tons of flour and thirty million blueberries. It was going to be huge." He nodded, finding his rhythm. "But when they went to bake it, they completely forgot they were indoors. The muffin just kept rising and rising, and there was nothing they could do to stop it. It smashed out the windows and pressed up against the roof and they all ran for their lives and then BOOM! The muffin blew up, and flour went everywhere, and it was a huge mess, and they didn't get in the Guinness Book of World Records. But they all got the day off and went home covered in flour."

Alex looked down at Nunu. "And that's why they look like that. The end."

Nunu just stared at him. For a second, he thought he'd lost her.

Then she laughed. "Boom."

Nice save, Alex thought to himself, and they continued on their way.

CHAPTER 26
The Man in the White Shirt

12:46 p.m.

The Man in the White Shirt ducked his head into the tiny grocery store. "Any chance I could use your phone? I lost mine back there somewhere."

The grocer tried the phone on the counter and then shook his head. "Everything's down." He reached into his pocket and held out his cell phone. "Here. Circuits have been jammed all morning, but maybe your luck's better than mine."

The Man in the White Shirt dialed; his fingers were shaking as he pressed the keys. For a long time, he heard nothing. Then the line came alive. He heard a click. His heart jumped into his throat.

But an instant later, a fast busy signal filled his ear.

"No luck," he murmured, and handed the phone back.

"Wait." The grocer held out a bottle of water.

The Man in the White Shirt fished in his pockets for change but came up empty.

The grocer waved him off and shoved the bottle into his hand. "Please."

Out on the sidewalk, the Man in the White Shirt opened the bottle of water and drank deeply. He hadn't realized how thirsty he'd become. He poured a little over his face and hands and began to wipe away the grit.

Something flopped to the ground behind him, landing with a hollow thump. He turned around to find a filthy gray bird flapping around on the pavement at his feet. It was struggling, unable to fly, its body and wings coated with grime. The Man in the White Shirt bent down with the bottle and poured water over the bird's body. The bird turned strangely calm, giving in, standing still as the dust ran off its feathers in dirty rivulets. When the bottle ran dry, the Man in the White Shirt stepped back.

A snow white dove now stood before him, glistening in the sun. The dove tested its wings with a couple of flaps, then soared away in a blinding flurry of white.

CHAPTER 27
Friends

1:07 p.m.

Mac snatched up the phone before the second ring.

"Bobby?" he blurted.

He tried to keep the disappointment out of his voice as he heard his oldest friend from his army days on the other end of the line, calling from California.

"Oh, hi Charlie."

Mac rubbed his eyes and paced back and forth in the kitchen.

"Nope. Nothing yet. Yeah, Tower 1, the North Tower. No, it fell second. Yeah, I'm sure. Maybe that gave him a little more time. I know. I can't either."

He glanced into the other room. Dottie was staring out the window, paying no attention to the nature documentary on her TV. Mac lowered his voice.

"No, she doesn't know; I doubt she'd understand anyway. But the pictures would get her too worked up. Listen, I should probably ring off, in case he tries to call."

He listened, nodding.

"I'll let you know as soon as I hear. Thanks for calling, Charlie." He swallowed hard as his voice cracked. "You're a good friend."

CHAPTER 28
Heroes

1:07 p.m.

"Hello, my friends, come in, come in," the pizza man said to the three small faces staring in from the sidewalk. A cloud of white dust puffed into the air as he slapped a ball of dough onto the counter and began kneading it into shape.

The pizza man was an Indian named Patel. ("An Indian from India," he always laughed.) Like everyone, he'd been glued to the news all day, watching on a tiny TV by the cash register. But now he flipped it off and waved them inside.

"Drink and a slice?"

Nunu nodded. Radar licked his chops.

Alex read the sign taped to the register: "Two slice + Coke = $5.95."

His stomach rumbled, but he shook his head. "No thanks."

"I'm hungry," whispered Nunu.

"We don't have any money," Alex mumbled.

Mr. Patel frowned. "I see. Not even a dollar?"

Alex shook his head again. Mr. Patel lifted his bushy black eyebrows.

"That is a shame. Because today the lunch special is two for one dollar."

Alex's stomach rumbled again.

"But," continued Mr. Patel, "the one dollar special comes with a one dollar rebate. Paid in advance. So, here you go. Your one dollar rebate."

He opened the till, plucked out a dollar, and handed it to Alex. Alex took it, confused.

"Ah, lunch for two, sir? That will be one dollar." Mr. Patel took the dollar from Alex's hand and put it back in the till. "Please sit anywhere you like."

The tiny restaurant was called Antonio's Pizza di Napoli. Mr. Patel had kept the name when he bought it from Antonio eighteen years ago. Alex settled them at a table by the window. The Indian pizza man didn't bat an eye as Radar followed them inside.

Mr. Patel brought over their slices, piping hot and fresh from the oven.

"Blow on it first," Alex told Nunu. "Or you'll burn your mouth."

Mr. Patel also set a bowl of meatballs on the floor for Radar, who sniffed them once, drooled, and buried his muzzle into the bowl.

Alex loved watching Radar eat. He loved everything about his dog.

But he knew if he ever hoped to see his father again, he had to take Radar home.

He wished there were another way.

Outside the window, a fire engine rolled slowly by. Alex counted six firefighters on the truck: four in the cab, and two on the running seats, facing backwards. As they passed, one of the backwards-facing firemen looked up and met eyes with Alex. Alex raised his hand in a little wave. The fireman waved back with a smile.

Alex wished he were a fireman right now.

Then he could be a hero and go rescue his dad.

Alex stared after the truck until it disappeared around a bend in the road.

"Can we have another?" Nunu asked, snapping him back to reality.

"Coming right up," Mr. Patel replied, and put two slices in the oven before Alex could say no.

"Thank you," said Alex.

Mr. Patel nodded seriously. "It is the least I can do."

CHAPTER 29
The Man in the White Shirt

2:33 p.m.

The Man in the White Shirt stared at the nurse.

He had gone far out of his way to get to the hospital, even though it would take him even longer now to make it home. But it was the thought of home that drove him here in the first place. Because it made him realize that as much as he needed his family, another family probably needed him more.

"I'm sorry," she repeated, "but the blood bank is closed. We're not taking any more donations."

"But I'm O-negative."

"Sir—"

"It's universal."

"I know, but we're full up. The bank can only handle a three-day supply."

"Should I wait?"

"For what?"

"You'll need more once you start going through it."

"We're not going through it," she said.

The nurse turned away quickly and began to shuffle through records like she was looking for something. The Man in the White Shirt stared at her back. It still didn't make any sense.

"But what about all the victims?"

"There aren't...." Her voice caught. "They haven't brought us any."

The man turned to the waiting room and saw what he'd missed before: there were no gurneys rolling through to the ER, no sick and wounded in pain. There wasn't a patient in sight.

And he knew then that none would be coming.

"You want to help out where you're needed most?" she asked.

He turned.

"Go home," she said quietly. "Go home."

CHAPTER 30
Dead End

3:10 p.m.

Alex's misdeeds flipped through his head like a slideshow as he thought about everything he'd done wrong that day: how he'd broken his promise to go straight home; how he'd disobeyed his parents and picked up a dog; how he'd been messing around in the park and lost track of Nunu; how he'd lied to his mother. And worst of all, how three words spoken in anger had put his father in danger.

He had to find Radar's home. It was the only way to set things right.

Radar dropped a stick at Alex's feet and jumped back in a crouch, ready for a game of fetch. He was still the same happy dog; he didn't know that Alex was about to give him away. Alex felt his ears go red as he flushed with shame.

He threw the stick, but it felt like a lie.

"Alex? How come we're not in school today?"

"'Cause we got off early."

Alex wished Nunu would stop asking him questions he was afraid to answer.

"Is Daddy coming home early?"

He didn't want to lie to her. He couldn't tell her the truth.

"Sure," he nodded.

"Yay." It was the tiniest cheer ever, simple and sweet. Alex hoped he could make his promise come true.

"Why are we stopping?"

Alex stared up at the street sign. His feet felt heavy and huge, like blocks of concrete.

"What does it say?" Nunu had followed Alex's gaze and was staring up at the street sign on the corner.

"Van Orton," he mumbled.

"What's that mean?"

Alex looked down the street of simple little frame houses, not so different from his own. He pulled out the piece of paper where the vet had written down Radar's address. He stared at it a long time.

"4 – 1 – 7," Nunu read. "What's that?"

"417 Van Orton Street. Radar's home."

Nunu frowned. "I thought he was going home with us." Radar pushed his big head against Alex's thigh. "He's your birthday dog."

Alex shook his head. "I have to make it right. I have to."

His view of the street turned blurry and wet. He blinked his vision clear and looked at Radar. The dog stared up at him with sad eyes, his tail hung low. One ear was folded back and plastered to a sticky corner of the bandage on his head. Alex knelt down beside him, gently peeled his ear free, and pressed the bandage back into place.

Then he threw his arms around the dog and pulled him close.

"I love you, boy," Alex whispered.

Radar licked Alex's cheek, wiping away the salty tears.

Nunu knelt down and hugged Radar, too.

Finally, Alex stood up. "C'mon." He waved at Radar to follow, his voice gruff. "Let's take you home." He lifted his heavy feet and forced himself to start down the street.

Radar didn't move.

"Radar. Let's go."

Radar sat down.

"I have to take you home. That's the deal. Let's go."

Radar lay down flat on the concrete.

Alex came back. He begged Radar to get up. He pleaded for him to follow.

Radar didn't budge.

Alex had to get this dog home. That was the deal. Desperate, he straddled the dog's back, slid his hands under his belly, and scooped him into his arms so fast that he took Radar by surprise. The dog was suddenly airborne, held aloft, paws sticking out. Alex pulled him tight against his chest while Radar kicked at the air in front of them.

"Stop fighting me!" Alex commanded, as he staggered forward.

That dog did not want to go down this street.

Nunu walked slowly ahead, sadly reading off the addresses. "411. 413. 415."

With Radar's back against his face, Alex couldn't see where he was going; he twisted his head so he could spot the curb beside them and then followed the sound of Nunu's voice. The closer they got, the harder Radar fought. It was the second time Alex had had to carry Radar today; his arms quivered from exhaustion, but he held on tight.

"417," said Nunu.

Radar gave a sudden lunge. He arched his back,

twisted free, and landed on all fours.

"RADAR!"

Alex expected him to hit the ground running. Instead, Radar circled around Alex and hid behind his legs.

Alex didn't want to look. He already hated this house.

"Alex?" Nunu tugged at his sleeve. Alex couldn't put it off any longer.

He turned to face the house at 417 Van Orton.

There was no house at 417 Van Orton.

Whatever had been there had burned to the ground. All that remained was a charred foundation, a few blackened timbers, and the remains of a teetering brick chimney propped up by a single two-by-four. A chain-link fence circled the lot, hung with "No Trespassing" signs every five feet.

Alex pressed against the fence; the sharp steel stung his fingers, but he held on tight as his world turned upside down again.

No! I did what I promised! he thought. I held up my end of the bargain! Bring the dog home, and Dad will be safe: that was the deal!

But how could he bring Radar home, if Radar had no home?

Radar raced along the fence until he found a narrow opening and squeezed through. Alex saw him too late.

"Radar, no. Get back here!"

"I'll get him," said Nunu, slipping easily through the hole in the fence.

"Nunu, get out! It's dangerous!"

She was inside before the words left his mouth. Alex dove after her and tried to squeeze under the fence, but he was too big. He clawed at the ground, pulling himself along in the dirt. The fence caught on his shirt. He was stuck, pinned on his belly.

"Freeze. Don't you move a muscle."

It was a man's voice. Alex didn't recognize it. And it didn't sound friendly. Alex twisted, trying to see behind him.

A surly old man stood above him, scowling down. His left hand hovered in his coat pocket.

"Come on out of there nice and slow."

Alex tried again but couldn't budge. "I can't move. I'm stuck."

"Good. That'll make it easier for the cops."

"No, wait. It's not my fault—"

"I'm sick and tired of you people always coming around to trash this place. And on a day like this. Can't you show any respect?"

"I'm just trying to—"

"How many more of you are there?"

Alex started to answer, then realized if the man had to ask, he hadn't seen Nunu. "Just me. I'm the only one." Alex hoped it sounded convincing.

And then Radar barked.

The old man looked up as the dog came bounding over, with Nunu at his heels. The man's expression changed completely.

"Is that Radar?"

CHAPTER 31
Van Orton Street

3:14 p.m.

"A bunch of druggies used to live there. They got evicted, so they trashed the place and bolted in the middle of the night. They dumped Radar out on the street like somebody's garbage."

The old man reached down and scratched Radar behind the ears, careful to avoid his bandage. Radar wagged his tail happily. Radar obviously knew the old man and liked him, so Alex breathed a little easier and figured the old man must be okay.

The old man opened the gate to his yard next door and ushered them through.

"Then a bunch more druggies got in there and

burned the whole place down. Almost took my house with it, but the fire trucks got here in time." He paused at the porch steps and glanced over at the empty lot. "This used to be a good neighborhood."

He turned sharply to Alex.

"You do drugs?"

Alex shook his head. The old man nodded approvingly and opened the front door. "Then come on in. I bet you kids could use a snack."

Radar darted right in like he owned the place.

Alex hung back. The old man looked at him curiously, then saw that Alex was staring at the man's coat pocket.

"Is that...?"

The old man laughed and slid the shiny black object out of his pocket.

"Remote control. I had the news on."

The house reminded Alex of his grandmother's. Everything inside was dark green and plaid. Little circles of lace draped the arms and backs of the sofa and chairs. The big oval rug in the entryway looked a little threadbare. It all felt familiar and oddly comforting.

"Call me Mac," said the old man, his voice suddenly quiet and gentle. "It's short for MacKnight. That's Mrs. Mac on the sofa."

"I'm Alex. That's my sister, Nunu. Guess you already know Radar."

Alex followed as Mac led them into the living room, where a tiny, stooped old lady sat on the sofa. She didn't look up as they entered. Her eyes were glued to the TV. It took Alex a minute to realize she was watching a pre-school cartoon, all bright colors and bubbly wubbly songs.

Mac bent down close to her and squeezed her shoulders softly. "We got company, Dottie. This is Nunu and Alex."

Dottie turned and noticed them. She broke into a wide smile, then reached out to pat Nunu on the head.

"Bunny!" she exclaimed, clapping her hands.

Then she looked right at Alex.

"Bunny," she said, seriously.

Her eyes were clear and green, but even Alex could tell she no longer knew what she was seeing. Dottie turned back to the TV and bobbed her head ever so slightly as the bouncy characters launched into another song.

"Have a seat," Mac said. "I'll go get us that snack."

Alex didn't know what else to do, so he took a seat and waited. Radar curled up at his feet. Nunu settled in between Alex and Mrs. Mac, then leaned over and whispered, "Is Gramma here?"

"Huh?"

"It smells like Gramma."

"It smells like perfume and old socks."

"Yep."

It didn't take long for Nunu to get sucked into the cartoon. Radar put his head on his paws and drifted off to sleep. Alex just sat there, at a loss. Where would he go next? What could he possibly do now?

He needed a new deal, but he was all out of ideas.

Alex heard a low voice murmuring in the next room. He slid off the end of the couch and followed the sound into the den. The voice was coming from a TV. The news was on. Alex paused in the doorway. From the side, he couldn't see the television clearly, and he wasn't sure he wanted to.

But he had to.

He took a deep breath and stepped through the door.

"To recap today's horrifying events: in what appears to be a coordinated series of attacks on major American institutions, three or possibly four commercial jets were hijacked by suspected terrorists this morning and deliberately crashed into buildings in New York and Washington.

"At approximately 8:45 a.m., American Airlines Flight 11, a Boeing 767 out of Boston, was hijacked and intentionally flown into the North

Tower of the World Trade Center in New York City. It struck around the 94th floor, and smoke and flames were immediately seen pouring from the building.

"Then at 9:03 Eastern time, a second 767, United Airlines Flight 175, also out of Boston, banked hard over New York Harbor and flew directly into the South Tower of the World Trade Center. It struck the south face of the building around the 80th floor, sending a fireball out the opposite side of the building.

"At approximately 9:40 a.m., a third plane crashed into the Pentagon in Washington, D.C. That plane, American Airlines Flight 77, left Washington Dulles this morning en route to Los Angeles but was apparently hijacked and turned back to complete its deadly mission.

"A fourth flight, United 93 out of Newark and bound for San Francisco, has crashed in a rural area in western Pennsylvania. Details are unclear now, but sources tell us the plane may well have had the White House as its target. We have also received reports that the passengers onboard United Flight 93 fought back and caused the plane to crash in an uninhabited area, preventing what could have been a much bigger tragedy.

"Then at about 10:00 this morning, the truly unthinkable came to pass, as all one hundred ten

stories of the South Tower of the World Trade Center completely collapsed, plummeting into the streets below. The North Tower continued to burn for another half hour; then it, too, completely collapsed. There were believed to be hundreds or possibly even thousands of workers and an unknown number of fire, police, and rescue personnel still trapped in the two buildings when they went down.

"Both collapses sent massive clouds of dust and debris roaring through the streets of lower Manhattan. All that remains of the Twin Towers is a smoldering pile of rubble that continues to burn fiercely at this hour, hampering rescue efforts.

"Other buildings around the World Trade Center have also been heavily damaged by the fires and the destruction of the Twin Towers. Fire officials tell us they believe the collapse of World Trade Center 7 is imminent.

"The death toll from today's events is unknown at this time but is expected to reach into the thousands."

Alex heard a cough behind him.

Mac stood in the doorway, holding a plate of cookies. The old man dug the remote out of his pocket and muted the volume.

"You didn't know?"

"I knew," said Alex.

But there's knowing, and then there's seeing. Seeing was a thousand times worse. Seeing made it real.

"They went down so fast," he said, his voice a whisper. "Is it true?"

"Of course it's true," Mac answered gruffly.

"No, I mean, there were people? Still inside?"

Mac nodded and looked away.

Alex felt weak. He sat down heavily on the couch. Tears rolled down his cheeks.

"He's not coming home," Alex whispered.

"What?"

"My dad."

Mac scowled. "You don't know that."

"Yes I do."

"No you don't. My own son was in the North Tower. And I expect him to come walking down this street any minute."

Alex shook his head. "Not my dad."

"Stop it," Mac barked.

"But he's not."

"Don't talk like that!"

"But it's true! You don't understand! I was supposed to give up Radar and take him home! But now I can't because he doesn't even have a home and if I can't take Radar home then my dad's not coming home! And it's all my fault!"

Mac stared at him. "You're making less sense

than Dottie, son."

"I told him...."

"Who?"

"My dad." Alex took an unsteady breath. "I told him, 'I hate you.'"

Alex's shoulders shook as he wrapped his arms around his legs and buried his face in his knees. Mac laid a hand gently on his shoulder and let him cry. Finally, he spoke up quietly.

"Son? Help an old man. What's all that got to do with Radar?"

Alex pulled his head up. "I already told you! I made a deal! If I take Radar home, then Dad will come home."

Mac nodded slowly. "You made a deal."

"I thought if I did a good thing, I could undo a bad thing."

Mac chuckled.

Alex scowled. "Don't laugh at me."

"Son, I'm only laughing because I've been doing the exact same thing all day."

Mac led the way back to the kitchen and found some tissues so Alex could blow his nose.

"My latest deal was to stop watching the phone. I convinced myself it wouldn't ring as long as I was staring at it. I thought if I could hold out for five minutes, then it would ring and it'd be my son. The longest I made it was thirty-one seconds."

"What's his name?"

"Bobby. He's an investment banker. You know what an investment banker does?"

Alex shook his head.

"Me neither. All I know is he moves money around."

"My dad moves people around," Alex said with a hint of pride. "He drives the PATH train to Manhattan."

"My son rides that train to work."

"My dad doesn't ride. He stands."

"He goes off every morning in a crisp white shirt. And every night he comes home wrinkled and pit-stained with his sleeves rolled up."

"That's just like my dad."

"I'd like to meet your dad."

"I'd like to meet your son."

"Bobby's our only one. A real sweet kid. Listen to me. 'Kid.' He's in his thirties. Probably about your dad's age, I guess." Mac's face clouded up. "He doesn't deserve...." His voice made a little choked sound. Alex understood.

Mac cleared his throat. "He volunteers at the soup kitchen downtown. Gives blood twice a year. After his mom started to slip, he moved back in to help me take care of her. He even gets us tickets to the ballgame a couple times a year."

"Yankee fan?" Alex motioned at Mac's cap.

"He dreams in pinstripes. You?"

"Yep. Me and my dad."

They were both quiet for a while. Mac broke the silence. "He was a good boy."

Alex looked sharply at Mac. "Is," he corrected him.

It took a second for Mac to realize what he'd said. Then he broke into a smile.

"You got your dad's number?"

Alex held up his cell phone.

"Let's give 'em another try."

Mac picked up the kitchen phone and dialed. Alex sat at the table with his cell phone and punched the speed-dial for his dad.

Mac put the phone to his ear, then brightened. "It's ringing."

Alex sat up straight. "Mine too."

CHAPTER 32
The Man in the White Shirt

3:34 p.m.

In a gutter in downtown Manhattan, half-buried under a piece of sheet metal, a lost cell phone buzzed to life.

But the Man in the White Shirt was no longer there to answer the call.

CHAPTER 33
Everything's Changed

3:35 p.m.

"No answer." Mac slowly hung up the handset.

"Me either." Alex closed his phone.

Neither one said anything for a minute.

"Why?"

It was Alex's turn to play the Why game.

"Why what?" Mac replied.

"Why did they do it?" asked Alex.

Mac chewed it over a long time.

"I don't know."

"How come the World Trade Center?"

Mac shrugged. "Big target."

"Do they hate us?"

"Looks like."

"Why?"

"Don't know."

"It doesn't make any sense."

"Nope. Things happen," Mac said. "They don't always make sense."

Mac glanced into the living room, where Dottie was snuggled up with Nunu, the two of them chatting like old friends about a cartoon on TV.

"We've had our share of tough times, Dottie and me. But she always had a phrase for times like this. Soon as I'd start bellyaching, she'd say, 'Better to light a candle than curse the darkness.'"

Alex thought about that. "What's that supposed to mean?"

"Damned if I know," Mac chuckled. "There's always bad stuff and good stuff in the world. I guess it means keep searching for the good."

"What's so good about today?"

Mac thought a moment. "You found Radar."

Alex pursed his lips. Okay, he thought. Maybe.

Radar came running in as he heard his name. Mac reached down and scratched the dog's ears. Radar's tail thumped against the chair legs. "Human beings have done evil things to each other for as long as there've been human beings. We also do kind things, too. Rescue a stray dog. Keep an old man company."

Alex thought about it some more, then shook his head.

"You don't want to keep me company?" asked Mac.

"No. I mean, yes. But...."

"But what?"

"But everything's changed," said Alex. He pointed at the TV in the other room. "That's what they said. After today, everything's changed."

Mac considered this for a while. Then he stood up and motioned for Alex to follow. They stepped out the front door and emerged into the shockingly bright sunshine. The air was warm, the sky cloudless and clear. Mac turned to Alex.

"What do you hear?"

Alex listened. "Birds."

"What else?"

"Cars. A dog."

"Sun still shining?"

"Yeah."

"Sky still blue?"

"Uh-huh."

"So tell me how everything's changed."

Alex chewed on his lip.

"It all depends on how you look at things," Mac continued. "When Dottie started to slip away, all I could see was what I was losing. Now I treasure every day with her."

Mac lowered himself onto the porch step. "Sometimes when a terrible thing happens, it can make a beautiful thing seem even more precious."

"But doesn't it make you mad, what happened to her?"

"I suppose I could be mad." He paused. "But what good would that do?"

Alex wanted to believe what Mac was saying.

"But what if...what if he's gone?"

Mac frowned. "Don't talk like that."

"But what if?"

"Didn't you hear a word I said?"

"But I might never see him again—"

Mac exploded. "That's enough, dammit!" He looked away, red-faced.

Alex jerked back, startled by Mac's outburst.

"I'm just scared he won't come home," Alex said quietly. "Aren't you?"

Mac nodded, blinking hard. "I can't lose Bobby, too," he whispered.

Alex watched in surprise as tears began to roll down the old man's face. He'd never seen an adult cry. He didn't know what to do, so he just reached his hand out and patted Mac gently on the shoulder. It must've been okay, because Mac put a hand over Alex's. They sat there in silence a very long time.

Alex looked up and down the street. It was just

like Mac said: everything looked so normal.

Then he noticed something new. He couldn't believe he hadn't spotted it yet.

"I know what's different," said Alex. "No planes."

Mac looked up at the empty sky. "You like planes?" he asked.

Mac led him around back to the garage and swung open the door, flooding the room with light. Alex couldn't believe his eyes. The entire place was filled with model planes. Biplanes and triplanes. Jets and turbo-props. Swept-wing fighters and bubble-nosed 747s. They lined the shelves and filled the corners and dangled from wires.

"Bobby always had a thing for planes. We used to build them together when he was a kid. We'd go up to the Palisades and fly them off the bluffs."

Alex walked slowly through the garage, staring up at the planes overhead.

"Sikorsky Flying Boat. P-51 Mustang. That's a Tiger Moth."

Mac was impressed. "You know your planes."

"I love planes," Alex said simply.

Mac laughed. "Mrs. Mac hated them! When Bobby moved to the city, she told me to clear out the planes so she could park her car in here. I told her the only thing I'd be clearing out was her side of the bed. Then she called me a big fat loser, and I called her a tight-lipped biddy. That's when she threw a skillet at my head."

"*Her*?" Alex glanced at the house, with the frail little woman inside.

"She was a corker," Mac explained.

"Did it hurt?"

"Only my feelings." Mac smiled at the memory. "I ducked. The wall didn't make out so good."

"Does she still...um...."

"Still what? Remember me?"

"Hate you."

Mac laughed. "She doesn't hate me! Never did. She's always loved me, and I love her right back."

"But she called you a big fat loser!"

"Listen to me, son. You can be mad at someone and still love 'em." Mac looked over to make sure Alex was listening. "Even when you say things you don't mean."

Alex thought of what he'd said to his dad. He hoped Mac was right.

Mac reached out to the nearest plane and spun the propeller.

"Hey. Wanna fly one?"

Out on the street, Mac guided the little gas-powered plane through a series of complicated aerial maneuvers. He did barrel rolls and wing-over-wing spins and even flew the plane straight down the street above their heads, inverted, then landed smoothly and taxied the plane right back to where they stood.

He held the controls out to Alex. "Your turn," he grinned.

Alex froze. He'd logged tons of hours on Screaming Eagles IV, but this was real. What if he messed up and wrecked Bobby's plane?

Mac leaned over to him. "Tower to Alex."

Alex came to. "A-Dawg."

"A dog?"

"It's my call sign."

Mac nodded and put the remote control into Alex's hand. "Tower to A-Dawg. You're cleared for take-off."

Alex throttled forward. The plane bumped along the pavement. He pulled back on the yoke. The plane lifted its nose and rose into the air. He trimmed the flaps.

The plane went into a nose-dive.

Mac never flinched. He reached over and flicked a lever to right the plane, then stayed next to Alex's side. Before long, Alex's flight-sim training kicked in, the wobbly plane straightened out, and he sent it circling overhead, soaring straight and true.

When it came time to land, Mac stood back and let him have the controls. Alex justified his vote of confidence with a picture-perfect one-touch land-ing. He gave the plane just enough juice to cruise to a stop and turn a 180 right at Mac's feet.

"Nice flying, A-Dawg."

"This is so much better than video," Alex grinned.

He stretched his arms and looked around and was surprised to see how late it had gotten. The shadows were getting longer, and the light was starting to fade in the east. He'd been so absorbed in flying that he'd even forgotten to be worried.

"Thanks, Mr. Mac."

"For what?"

Alex shrugged.

"My pleasure, son."

"I better get going."

"Already? You're welcome to wait here. You don't take up much room."

"I promised I'd get Nunu home." Alex checked the time on his cell phone. "Six hours ago."

Mac sighed. "I understand," he said quietly.

Mac bent over to pick up the plane. Alex could tell he was disappointed. For a while, they'd been able to forget their troubles and just have fun, and neither of them wanted it to end just yet. As Mac stood up with the plane, Alex put a hand on his arm.

"One more?"

Eleven

Mac broke into a broad smile.

The model aircraft sped down the street for one last run. Then with a dip of the flaps, the wheels left the ground, and Alex shaded his eyes and stared up into the sky as the little plane found the wind and began a slow, steady climb.

CHAPTER 34
The Man in the White Shirt

6:02 p.m.

The Man in the White Shirt saw it first, streaking in from the northwest. He watched it bank sharply and head straight for them. Within seconds, people around him saw it, and before long, everyone on the bridge had turned to look.

An anxious murmur ran through the crowd.

A woman beside him gave a frightened gasp. "Oh no," she whispered.

The Man in the White Shirt put a comforting hand on her elbow.

"It's okay," he reassured her. "It's an F-15. It's one of ours."

The needle-nosed jet rocketed past, twin engines screaming. The roar was deafening. The woman threw her hands over her ears. They watched as it flew straight down the length of the island, so low it seemed to barely skim the tops of the skyscrapers.

As it cleared the tip of Manhattan and raced out over the harbor, the woman finally breathed a sigh of relief.

"How did you know?" she asked.

"I know planes," he shrugged.

The woman left him with a grateful nod, then fell back in with the crowd making its way across the George Washington Bridge, the massive suspension bridge connecting Manhattan to New Jersey. Normally, the bridge delivered thousands of cars and trucks into New York every day. Now, all traffic into the island had been blocked; everyone on the bridge was headed away—headed home.

The Man in the White Shirt lingered a moment on the bridge, staring after the plane as it continued on beyond the skyline, dragging a white vapor line behind it like a string. It was the first plane he'd seen all day, and he couldn't take his eyes off it. He watched as it receded into the distance, growing smaller and smaller until it seemed to just float there, frozen in place, like a model plane hanging from a wire.

Just like home, he thought. He felt a twinge of guilt; he had no business staring at planes when the ones who depended on him were still waiting.

He turned away and continued his long march home.

CHAPTER 35
Faces

6:37 p.m.

Alex stared out the bus window, searching the faces on the street. He was looking for his father, hoping to spot him in the crowd, making his way home. He knew it was a long shot. Right now, his dad could be anywhere.

Even at Ground Zero.

He couldn't stop thinking about it: the planes hitting; the billowing smoke; the towers as they fell. He closed his eyes, but that only made it worse. The fireball. The smoke. The collapse. Over and over on a constant loop in his brain.

He blinked and wiped a tear off his cheek.

He heard sniffling and looked around. He wasn't the only one on the bus crying quietly.

Something cool and wet brushed his hand. It was Radar, licking the salty drop off his fingers. Alex gazed down at Radar.

Greatest. Dog. Ever.

When Alex looked back up, he caught eyes with a woman across the aisle. She wore a hotel maid's uniform, gray with a white collar. Her shoulders were hunched, her brow creased. But when her gaze connected with Alex's, her eyes went soft, and she gave him a tiny smile.

Alex looked around at the other passengers. He and Nunu rode the bus all the time, and he was used to seeing what they called "bus face," the blank stare most riders wore to avoid making eye contact with the people around them. He sometimes played a game with Nunu where they'd each put on their best bus face and see who could hold it the longest, staring ahead like wide-eyed zombies until one of them (usually Nunu) lost it and got the giggles.

But today was different. Everyone looked kind of sad; some kept their gaze on the floor, others watched intently out the window. But there was no sign of bus face anywhere. Then it happened again: he caught eyes with a man in a suit; the man nodded and gave him a little smile. Incredible. Four times in one day. And that didn't even count the bus driver, who didn't give him any trouble about bringing Radar on board.

Alex felt a tap on his shoulder and jerked around, startled. It was the lady in the seat behind him, a middle-aged Hispanic woman in a flowered dress. She was holding up his Gameboy.

"It fell out of your bag."

"Oh. Thanks."

She gave him a kind smile and turned away.

That makes five, Alex thought to himself.

Nunu watched him put away the Gameboy and then went back to reading the picture book in her lap. Alex turned back to the window. Down a side street, he saw a boy about his age burst out his front door, sprint down the sidewalk, and jump into the arms of a man getting out of a car.

Alex watched for as long as he could, until the bus went through a short tunnel. For a brief moment, there was nothing but darkness beyond the window, and Alex's face was suddenly reflected back to him in the glass.

He saw the wet streak on his cheek and looked away, embarrassed.

The bus pulled over at the next stop. Radar stiffened, back straight, ears pricked. He growled.

Alex followed Radar's eyes: it was Calvin, one of Jordan's goons, coming down the aisle. Alex sat up.

He didn't know why, but he didn't feel scared. Something was different about Calvin. Then it hit him: Calvin wasn't smirking or cracking his knuckles or trying to act tough. He just looked like a regular kid.

Calvin froze when he spotted Alex. Alex stared back. Calvin broke his gaze and looked away, then down at Radar, whose bandaged ear twitched back and forth.

"Uhhh...he okay?"

"Yeah."

Calvin shifted his weight from one foot to the other, his eyes on the floor.

"We didn't mean to hurt him."

Alex shook his head.

"Yes, you did."

"Yeah." Calvin nodded. "Sorry."

Seriously? thought Alex. An apology? From Calvin? He considered pinching himself to see if he was dreaming, but he played it cool and just nodded.

Then Calvin surprised him again. "Jordan's a jerk sometimes."

"All the time."

"Yeah."

Alex noticed a purplish bruise on Calvin's cheek and remembered something from earlier that day. Just before Jordan threw the bottle, Alex saw him take a swing at Calvin and shove him aside. A completely crazy thought occurred to Alex: had Calvin been trying to stop Jordan from throwing the bottle?

Alex pointed at Calvin's cheek. "Jordan give you that?"

Calvin was silent a long time. "Yeah," he mumbled. "I, uh, tried..." said Calvin, his voice trailing off.

Amazing.

"Why do you hang out with him?" asked Alex.

Calvin shrugged. "Who else am I gonna hang out with?"

Alex knew it was true. He studied Calvin's face. Calvin's gaze was still glued to the floor; he couldn't look Alex in the eye. Both of them were unsure what the next move should be. They might've stayed that way all night if Alex hadn't suddenly noticed the street signs outside. He reached over and yanked the bell cord, then nudged Nunu, who put away her picture book.

"My stop," said Alex.

Calvin stepped aside to let them pass.

"See you tomorrow, I guess," said Calvin.

Alex shrugged. "Whatever." Then something inside him made him stop. He didn't like the way that sounded. He turned back towards Calvin.

"Hey, Calvin. Your family okay? After...you

know...."

Calvin looked surprised; then he nodded. "Yeah."

Alex hustled Radar and Nunu to the door while Calvin continued down the aisle. Halfway to the back, Calvin turned around and called to Alex.

"What about yours?"

But Alex was already gone. The doors closed with a hiss, and the bus moved on.

CHAPTER 36
The Man in the White Shirt

7:12 p.m.

The Man in the White Shirt picked up his pace as he saw the buses lined up in the commuter lot, engines idling at a low rumble. He walked down the row until he found the one he was looking for: Jersey City. Home.

But as the doors to the bus hissed open, the Man in the White Shirt held back.

Next to the parking lot stood a pay phone, with twenty people waiting to use it.

He'd been trying to call home all day but hadn't been able to get through. He was anxious to reach his family, to let them know he was okay.

Passengers jostled past him and climbed onto the bus, eager to get home. The Man in the White Shirt stood there. He'd been moving all day, on the run, never stopping. Now he was paralyzed, unable to make up his mind.

"You comin'?" the bus driver asked sharply. He sounded impatient and tired. It had been a long day for him, too.

The Man in the White Shirt looked from the bus to the pay phone.

"On or off, mack. I ain't got all night."

The Man in the White Shirt made up his mind. He headed for the phone. There would be more buses.

"STOP THE BUS!"

The Man in the White Shirt saw an older, heavy-set woman limping towards him and waving her arms like a broken windmill. He turned and sprinted after the bus, which had just edged away from the curb. He caught up with it and smacked his palm on the door. The bus jerked to a halt. The door flung open, nearly hitting him in the face.

"Wait," he told the driver.

The bus driver scowled. But he waited.

"Thank you," the limping woman gasped, out of breath, as the Man in the White Shirt boosted her up the bus steps and helped her down the aisle to an empty row.

The instant she was settled, the bus lurched and pulled away. The Man in the White Shirt staggered and turned to glare at the driver, who shot him a challenging look in the mirror. The Man in the White Shirt felt the blood rise into his face. After all he'd been through, why should he have to put up with this jerk?

But then he took a deep breath, exhaled, and settled into an empty row. He'd kept it together this far; no reason to lose it now. The phone call would have to wait. He sat back, closed his eyes, and let the bus carry him south.

CHAPTER 37
Sunshine

7:12 p.m.

The sun was just going down as Alex turned the corner onto his block. By the time he reached his front door, his legs were quivering and his arms were about to fall off. Nunu had completely run out of steam a half block from the bus stop, so Alex carried her the rest of the way home. With his backpack on his back and Nunu in his arms in front like a papoose, he looked like an apple with legs.

Radar trotted beside them carrying Nunu's backpack, the handle clenched in his teeth, always careful to keep his head up so it wouldn't scrape the ground.

As Alex fished in his pocket for his key, he noticed little details around the porch: the broken front step where he'd fallen and knocked out his first baby tooth; the loose rail Nunu loved to climb on to jump into her daddy's arms; the bushes in front where he and Dougie and Kwan had piled up used Christmas trees last winter to make a fort. He noticed the peeling paint on the shutters that his dad had repainted just last year, and the brown stain on the driveway where his mom had tried to refinish an old table. He took it all in, the big elm tree and the dying rosebush, the freshly mowed lawn and the missing shingle by the chimney, the darkened windows and the warm glow of the porch light.

It felt good to be home.

Nunu roused as he lowered her to the ground. She rubbed her eyes with one hand and her nose with the other.

Alex eased the front door open. Inside, the house was dark.

"Anybody home?" he called out.

Silence answered back.

Nunu took her backpack from Radar and dropped it in the front hall. "Where's Mommy and Daddy?" she asked.

"Not home yet."

Alex was halfway to the bathroom when he realized that Radar hadn't followed them inside. The dog hung back on the porch, skittish and unsure of himself. He kept approaching the doorway and then jumping back. Alex waved him in.

"C'mon, boy. That's it."

Radar whimpered and paced back and forth but wouldn't come in.

Nunu reappeared. "What's the matter with him?"

Alex thought about the house that Radar came from, or what was left of it. No wonder the dog didn't trust houses.

"He's just a little scared," said Alex.

"There's nothing to be scared of, Radar," Nunu said. Then she walked onto the porch, put her hands on his butt, and gave him a great big push.

Radar shot through the door and skidded across the floor. While he scrambled to get his footing, Alex quickly shut the door behind Nunu so he couldn't run away. Radar stood stock still, nose twitching as he sniffed the air.

"What do you think?" asked Alex.

Radar gave one loud bark of approval, whacked the wall three times with his tail, then bolted straight for the living room, sniffing everything he passed on the way.

"I think he likes it," Nunu smiled.

Alex made a beeline for the bathroom because,

well, they'd been gone a really long time. When he came back out, Radar had made himself right at home and was stretched out across the big lounge chair in the living room.

"Hey, that's my dad's chair. Out."

Alex motioned for Radar to move. The dog climbed up over the arm and dropped onto the couch.

Nunu flopped down next to him and reached for the remote. Alex realized what would be on every channel that night. He stepped quickly in front of the TV.

"Chores, Nunes."

"I'm tired."

"You know the rule. Chores before dinner."

Nunu moaned and slid off the front of the sofa.

"Who's gonna cook dinner?" she asked, shuffling off to the kitchen.

Alex hadn't thought of that. He headed to the kitchen after her.

Behind him, Radar sat up, waited till the coast was clear, then climbed across the arms of the sofa and straight back into the big, comfy chair.

Alex's mom kept a tiny TV on the kitchen counter next to the stove. Alex waited as Nunu pulled an empty garbage bag from under the sink and headed back to the bedrooms to collect the trash. Then he flicked on the TV to catch the latest news on the disaster, keeping one eye on the hot dogs he was frying and one eye out for Nunu. But the stations didn't have much new to report, and watching the towers fall again and again wasn't making him feel any better, so he turned it off.

Suddenly, Alex heard voices in the other room. He dropped the pan with a clang and went sprinting into the living room.

But it was only the TV. Radar had stepped on the remote. Alex flicked off the TV, then motioned for Radar to vacate his dad's lounge chair.

"Radar, out."

Radar tucked his tail and slinked off the chair. Alex tugged him by the neck to the other side of the room and settled him in the corner; then he headed back in to finish dinner. Radar followed him with his eyes all the way out the door.

Back in the kitchen, Alex found a box of instant macaroni and cheese and tried to follow the recipe on the back. When everything in the pot turned safety-vest orange, he figured he'd done it right. Satisfied, he licked the extra cheese dust out of the creases in the packet.

While he was cooking, the phone rang. Alex snatched it up quickly.

"Hello?"

"Hey, Alex."

"Oh. Hey, Dougie." Alex tried to hide his disappointment. "What's up?"

"Kwan and me, we, uh...." Doug's voice trailed off. He got a running start and tried again. "Sorry we ditched you."

"You had to. It was Jordan. Every man for himself."

"Nah. That wasn't cool," said Dougie, sounding relieved.

"Don't worry about it. You guys get away okay?"

"Yeah, but what happened?"

"Radar—oh, that's my dog's name, by the way."

"Awesome name."

"Jordan was about to pulverize me when Radar snuck up behind him and growled."

"No way."

"You should've seen the look on Jordan's face."

"I can't believe I missed it! I have no life."

"Radar was like this total hero. He chased them all the way out of the park. They were screaming like babies the whole time."

"Did he bite him? Please tell me there was blood."

"Tore his back pocket off."

"Epic!"

They both laughed until they fell into an awkward silence.

"You see the news?" Dougie asked quietly.

"Yeah," said Alex. "Your mom and dad home?"

"Yeah. Yours?"

"Not yet."

Silence crackled on the line. Alex swallowed hard, a sudden lump in his throat.

"Thanks for calling, Dougie. Talk to you tomorrow."

"Yeah. Later."

Alex hung up the phone and turned off the burners on the stove.

"Dinner's ready," he called, then smiled as Radar came padding in. Alex was about to drop a hot dog on the floor for him, but Radar caught it in mid-air and hoovered it down in one gulp, then looked expectantly at Alex to see what came next.

Radar got four more hot dogs that evening, while Alex and Nunu gobbled down their mac-and-cheese and hot dogs almost as fast as Radar. When they finished dinner, Alex wet the corner of his napkin in his glass and wiped Nunu's face, just like his mother always did.

After dinner, Alex cleaned the pots and plates (with a little help from Radar's tongue), while Nunu got her PJs on. Alex figured she'd put up a fight about bedtime, but Nunu was too tired to argue. She could barely stop yawning long enough to brush her teeth.

Alex followed Nunu into the bedroom and over to her pink bed. There were dolls lying over the flight line, but he let it go. It didn't seem like such a big deal anymore.

Nunu yawned and climbed into bed. Alex shut off the light, then pulled up the covers and tucked her in.

Nunu yawned again. "When's Mommy coming home?"

"Soon."

"And Daddy?"

Alex hesitated.

"Soon," he replied.

"Alex? Are you sad?"

The question took him by surprise. Nunu was watching him with a serious expression.

I guess I'm still no good at keeping my feelings off my face, he thought.

"A little," he answered.

"I know."

"You do?" How could she know? He'd tried so hard to protect her from the terrifying news that day.

Nunu nodded gravely. "Mommy and Daddy forgot your birthday."

Alex exhaled a sigh of relief.

Nunu frowned. "I'm mad at them."

"Don't be mad."

"But I am."

"Please, Nunu. Please don't be mad at them. I'm

not. See? They didn't forget. They're just running late. They'll be here soon. Okay?" He pulled the covers up. "Now just go to sleep."

She kicked them off. "No. I'm not sleepy."

Alex laughed. "Yes, you are."

"No."

"You haven't stopped yawning since we got home."

She shook her head and rubbed her eyes.

"But it's bedtime," he pleaded.

"NO," she said firmly.

"C'mon, Nunes. Just go to sleep."

"NO! You can't tell me what to do! You're not Daddy!"

Then she burst into tears and buried her head in the pillow.

"I want Daddy..." she wailed.

Alex felt totally overwhelmed. He sat on the edge of the bed, nervously bouncing his leg and holding his ears in frustration. He wanted to run away. He wanted Nunu to stop crying. He wanted his dad to come home. He wanted everything to be back to normal.

Then it hit him: that's all Nunu wanted, too.

Alex remembered what their father always did at bedtime. He closed his eyes and pictured his dad just home from work, sitting on the edge of Nunu's bed, the sleeves of his wrinkled white shirt rolled up, his strong hands working their magic as they led Nunu into sleep.

Alex opened his eyes. He reached out, just like his father, and quietly began to stroke Nunu's head. Nunu shifted on her pillow, unburying her face. Alex continued to brush her hair with his fingers, drawing his hand across her forehead in long, slow strokes, barely touching her, as soft as if he were petting a baby bird. Nunu's breathing began to slow. Alex leaned down close to her ear.

And then, quiet as a whisper, Alex began to sing.
"You are my sunshine, my only sunshine
"You make me happy, when skies are gray.
"You'll never...."

He paused, waiting for her to chime in. This was always her favorite part. But Nunu had drifted off.

So Alex sang it for her.
"...know, dear, how much I love you.
"Please don't take my sunshine away."

Then he bent down and kissed Nunu softly on the head.

CHAPTER 38
Night

8:31 p.m.

Mac stood at the kitchen counter waiting for the coffee to brew. It was his fourth pot of the day. The doctors had told him to lay off the caffeine, but he figured they'd make an exception for today.

He breathed in the steam, thinking back to the first pot of the morning. He pictured Bobby coming into the kitchen in his crisp white shirt, sleeves unbuttoned, jacket slung over his arm. They drank their coffee in comfortable silence, the way they always did, Mac with the Sports section, Bobby reading Business. Then Bobby checked his watch, stood up, and shrugged on his coat.

"See ya tonight, Pop."

And then he was gone.

The coffeemaker beeped. Mac opened his eyes and poured himself a cup. From behind the counter, he had a perfect view out the window to the corner at the end of the street. Before dementia clouded her mind, Dottie used to sit at the counter and watch for Bobby to come around that corner on his way home from work. Mac used to tease her about it, but the truth is he'd do the same thing, finding excuses to be in the kitchen so he could sneak a peek over her shoulder as he came and went.

Mac stared out the window for the hundredth time that day, then closed his eyes and tried to conjure up the scene—Bobby, coming around the corner, stepping into the yellow glow of the street lamp, the light on his white shirt like a ray of sunshine. Mac kept his eyes closed, trying to hold onto the image, trying to make it come true.

He realized he was making deals again. He didn't care.

"Where's Robert?"

Mac spun around so fast he spilled his coffee. Dottie was standing in her nightgown in the middle of the living room, gazing around with a troubled, quizzical expression. The house had been so quiet he'd almost forgotten she was back there.

"Hey there, kiddo. What are you doing up?" he asked quietly.

Dottie turned and looked at him. Mac couldn't tell if she still recognized him or not, but she allowed him to lead her back down the hall to the bedroom. He pulled back the covers and helped her swing her legs up and into bed. She still seemed agitated, so he sat with her and stroked her hand, which always calmed her.

But not tonight.

"Where's Robert?" she asked again.

Mac swallowed hard and looked out the window.

"He's on his way home."

CHAPTER 39
Vigil

8:31 p.m.

The Man in the White Shirt was the last one off the bus. As he stepped down to the street, he turned back to the driver and nodded.

"Have a safe night," he said.

"Um, yeah," the driver mumbled. "You too," he added, a little more brightly.

The driver waited for him to cross in front of the bus before pulling slowly away from the curb and heading off in the other direction. Before long, the bus rounded a curve and vanished from sight.

The Man in the White Shirt was surprised by how quiet it was, so close to the center of town. The streets were empty, the restaurants closed. Then he realized why: everyone had gone home.

As he turned down a lane full of small, tidy houses, he could see lights on in every window, and people sitting in those windows, looking up and down the street. Neighbors huddled in small groups on the sidewalk. Old men sat on their porches. He felt their eyes searching him as he passed, trying to place him, to see if they knew him.

Everywhere he looked people were watching, waiting.

Sitting vigil.

Mac sat on his porch stoop, nursing a mug of coffee that had long ago gone cold. Beside him sat the model plane he'd been flying that afternoon. He idly spun the propeller as he glanced up at the street corner.

Still nobody there.

Then he heard footsteps, coming from the other direction.

He leaned forward. The street was darker at that end, and he squinted into the shadows. He could just make out the silhouette of a person, coming closer. But as they passed in front of his house, he saw it was a woman, the lawyer who lived four doors down. She waved. He waved and forced a smile, trying to hide his disappointment.

Then he settled back on his elbows again to wait.

Alex pushed the curtains back and peered out the front window again.

Still nobody.

Behind him, Radar whimpered. Alex watched him circle the big lounger again, sniffing at it furiously and whining in frustration. He'd been calm after dinner, but now he was agitated again, pacing and whining constantly.

"I told you, that's Dad's chair."

Alex started toward the living room, ready to defend the chair again, but Radar pushed past him and hurried to the front door. He pawed the door and scratched at the frame, still whimpering like mad.

"Ohhhh. Gotta go, boy?" Suddenly, it made sense.

Radar whimpered again.

Alex unlocked the door and swung it open for Radar to go do his business.

The second the door opened, Radar bolted.

"NO!"

Alex took out after Radar, but the dog shot away like a rocket. He bounded across the yard at top speed, jumped the neighbor's hedge, then hit the ground and kept on going. Alex chased him to the corner, but Radar was already long gone, blocks away and out of sight.

Just like that.

"Radar. RADAR!!"

No way, thought Alex. What happened?? It can't be over. I can't lose him, just like that. He looked back at the house, where he could see the light from inside spilling out his front door. He couldn't just let Radar go. But he couldn't leave his sister alone.

"RA - DARRRR!!!"

Alex stood on the corner, listening for a bark, a whine, anything. He listened until his shout died off into echoes.

And then there was nothing. Silence.

Radar was gone, vanished into the darkness.

The Man in the White Shirt detoured into the big city park. He figured the shortcut would save him nearly a half-hour.

What he hadn't counted on was that it would be so dark. Usually, there were ball games out here under the lights; but tonight, the fields were empty, the lights out. He didn't want to admit it, but half-way through the park, he got a little spooked.

He was crossing the baseball field at the edge of the woods when he heard something moving through the brush. He froze, listening.

Ten yards away, he saw a figure emerge from the woods.

A dog.

No collar. Probably a stray. The Man in the White Shirt didn't move a muscle. The dog saw him anyway. It paused, staring back. It was big and had some kind of bandage on its ear. It cocked its head, watching him, then loped away.

The Man in the White Shirt breathed a sigh of relief, chuckling at his own jumpy nerves, and continued on his way.

Alex felt numb. He still couldn't believe that Radar was gone.

So he tried not to think about it and got busy cleaning the kitchen. He wiped down the table and vacuumed under Nunu's chair. He dried the dishes and put them away in the cabinet. He scooped the leftovers into a plastic bin and opened the refrigerator to stow them inside.

And came to a complete halt.

There, on the bottom shelf, sat his birthday cake. The one his mom had made for tonight. "Tower to A-Dawg," it read, in green icing, "Happy

Birthday!!!"

Alex had been told a zillion times not to stand there with the refrigerator door open, but he couldn't help it. He stared at the cake as an idea slowly took shape in his mind. When he was sure what he wanted to do, he slammed the door and headed off with purpose.

He was a man with a plan.

He hurried to the pantry and found the bag of birthday decorations his mom had bought. He grabbed some scissors and tape, dumped the decorations on the kitchen table, and got to work.

Twenty minutes later, the job was done. The banner was complete.

He carried the banner into the living room and stood on a kitchen chair to pin it to the drapes. When it was hanging straight, he stepped back to examine the finished product.

Behind him, a key slid into the front door.

Alex spun around.

The door swung open.

And there stood his mom.

She took two steps into the room, then stopped short, taking in Alex and the banner and the TV news in the background, and she knew he knew everything.

"Oh, Alex," she said, as she pulled him into her arms and started to cry.

The Man in the White Shirt kept up a steady pace now as he crossed the tall bridge that stretched over a railroad yard and a narrow river. He paused briefly in the center, the highest point, where he could see all the way to Manhattan, glittering like a jewel right down to its southern tip, which remained dark, and empty.

Then he lowered his head and pushed on.

Mac paced the living room, clutching the remote tightly in his fist. The walls flicked from black to blue to black to blue as he ticked through the TV channels, one after another after another.

But the story was always the same.

Alex's mom sat on the sofa, the light from the muted TV flickering on her face. She was still in her nurse's uniform; she hadn't even bothered to change. After checking on Nunu, who was still asleep, she had collapsed on the couch with her arm around Alex. They hadn't said much since she'd been home. They'd just held onto each other.

"Mom?"

She thought he'd fallen asleep.

"Yes?"

"Why didn't you tell me?"

She paused a long time before answering. Then she told him the truth.

"I didn't think you could handle it."

She looked around her, at the dishes drying in the kitchen, the banner hanging on the curtain, the door to the bedroom where Nunu was sleeping, safe and sound.

"I guess I was wrong."

The Man in the White Shirt was close now. A car zoomed past him and stopped hard in front of a house up the block. A man in his fifties jumped out of the car with the speed of a guy half his age and ran to the front porch, taking the steps two at a time as someone inside flung open the front door, bathing him in golden light.

The Man in the White Shirt smiled to himself, knowing he would be there soon.

Mac picked up the phone and dialed again. Someone once told him the definition of insanity is doing the same thing over and over, expecting a different result. But Mac knew he'd go crazy if he didn't keep trying.

So he dialed again and put the phone to his ear, waiting to hear his son's voice.

The Man in the White Shirt saw the street sign lit up by the street lamp on the corner, and his heart jumped into his throat.

He turned the corner and picked up his pace.

Then he broke into a run.

Alex and his mom slumped on the sofa, leaning into each other like two poles of a teepee, holding each other up, both asleep.

The Man in the White Shirt sprinted across the lawn and up onto the porch. He tried the door, but it was locked. He searched his pockets. He'd lost his keys.

The Man in the White Shirt laughed to himself: all this way, and he was locked out of his own house. He lifted his arm and knocked sharply on the door.

Mac stood up and crossed to the front door. He pulled the door open.

And then he peered out into the empty night. He took a step onto the porch and looked up toward the corner again. But there was nobody there.

CHAPTER 40
Home

9:27 p.m.

Alex flung open the front door.

The Man in the White Shirt broke into a wide grin and threw open his arms.

Alex leapt onto his father's chest. He wrapped his legs around his dad's back and buried his face in his neck and hung on like he'd never let go.

Alex's mom came running onto the porch right behind him and threw her arms around both her guys. Squeezed between them, Alex felt warm and safe for the first time all day. Together, they rocked back and forth in silence. They could have stayed that way all night. Alex wouldn't have minded.

Finally, his dad cleared his throat and whispered huskily into Alex's neck.

"Hi, pal."

"Hi, Dad."

Alex closed his eyes as his dad planted a long kiss on the top of his head.

"Got one of those for me?" asked his mom.

"I've got a thousand," said his dad, covering her face in kisses.

They stumbled inside, carrying each other along. And then Alex's dad came to a complete stop, staring at the banner Alex made, strung across the living room wall.

It read: WELCOME HOME, DAD.

"He did it himself," said his mom.

Alex saw his dad swallow hard, unable to speak.

"And he cooked dinner, and did the dishes, and took out the trash," she went on. "I'm proud of you, young man."

Young man.

Alex liked how that sounded.

"He even put Nunu to bed," she added.

"DADDY!!!!!!"

"Come here, you little monkey!" he shouted, as Nunu hopped down the stairs in her pajamas and ran to his arms.

"You're dirty, Daddy," said Nunu, as he scooped her up.

"You're right, and I'm gonna get it ALL OVER YOU!" Nunu giggled and twisted as her daddy rubbed his head on her tummy. Only then did Alex notice that Nunu was right: their dad was covered in soot and grime. His face was streaked with dirt; there were pieces of gravel buried in his hair. And his white shirt and black pants looked like they'd decided to meet in the middle at gray.

"Dad, are you okay?" asked Alex.

"I'm fine. We got out in time."

Alex nodded. He should've felt relief, should've felt elation. But something was still bothering him.

"Dad?"

"Yeah, pal."

Alex forced himself to look his father in the eye. "I'm sorry about what I said last night." He lowered his gaze and stared at his sneakers. "I didn't mean it."

"I know, Alex. I always knew."

Alex looked up. "How?"

"It's a dad's job to know."

His dad's smile was warmer than an August sun.

"I love you, Dad."

"I love you too, pal."

Both of them sniffled as the tears rolled down their cheeks, neither one the least bit embarrassed.

Alex's dad stood at the kitchen counter wolfing down Alex's hot dogs and macaroni-and-cheese like a starving man, which he was. He hadn't eaten a single thing since breakfast.

"Mmmmm! Alex, this is amazing. You could teach your mom a thing or two."

She smacked him on the butt with a dish towel.

"So how'd you get home?" asked Alex.

"Walked. A lot," said his dad, following their mom as she brought his food to the table and made him sit down. After shoveling down another mouthful, he continued.

"I even cut through the park to get home faster."

"Honey! You know that park's not safe at night!"

"Don't worry. There was nobody there," he reassured her. "Just a dog."

Alex sat up straight. "A dog?"

The words had barely left his mouth when, outside the front door, a dog barked.

Alex thought he was imagining things.

By the second bark, he knew it was real.

Out on the front porch, something was barking and whining and thumping like a drum against the front door.

Alex came out of his chair like a shot. For the second time that night, he ran to the door and flung it open—and was instantly flattened by Radar, who pounced on his chest and started licking his face from top to bottom.

"RADAR!" Nunu ran up and gave him a big hug. Her arms barely reached around his neck.

"Down boy!" Alex laughed, pushing the dog off. As Alex stood up, his father came slowly to his side, his mouth hanging wide open.

"Holy cow. That's the same dog," said his dad. "He had a bandage on his ear, just like that. He must've followed me home from the park."

Alex knew better. He was sure Radar had found his dad and made sure he got home safely. "I bet he was watching out for you."

Alex's mom put her hands on her hips. "Would someone please explain to me what's going on?"

Alex handled the introductions. "Mom, Dad. Meet Radar."

"It's his birthday dog," Nunu chimed in.

"Nunes!"

Alex now found both his parents staring at him with interest.

"Okay. The thing is, I found him. On the way home. And then I tried to give him back. And then he ran away. It's a long story."

"You brought home a stray dog?" repeated his mom.

"I wanted to keep him. But he belonged to someone else. The vet told me where he lived, so I tried to take him home."

"But his house was burned," Nunu explained.

"The vet?" asked their dad. "What vet?"

"Radar was trying to protect us and chased away these bullies who wanted to beat me up, but then they threw a bottle at him and hit him on the head."

Wrapped up in his tale, Alex didn't seem to notice his parents' befuddled, slightly horrified expressions as they tried to follow along.

"So I took him to the vet. That's where he got the bandage. But he kinda scraped it off when he scrunched under the fence in front of the druggie house that burned down."

Alex's dad's mouth opened and shut, like he wanted to ask something but couldn't figure out which one of his thirty-eight questions to start with.

Meanwhile, Alex's mom's nursing instincts kicked in. She bent down to check on Radar's bandage. "You okay, big guy? You took care of my babies?"

She laughed as Radar licked her hand with his meaty tongue. She scratched his neck, and Radar's tail whacked away at the wall like a jackhammer, and that just made her laugh even harder, and then Alex knew everything was going to be all right.

Across town, Mac came in and closed the front door behind him. He'd been sitting on the porch, watching the street, until he'd finally grown too chilly. As he passed through the kitchen, he glanced out the window at the empty street corner once more, then put another pot of coffee on and settled back in to wait.

He would wait all night and all the next day.

But Mac's son would never come home.

The next morning, Alex's mom made his favorite birthday breakfast for the second day in a row.

The trains to lower Manhattan were still shut down, so his dad had the day off. As the four of them tucked into their pancakes, Radar sat at Alex's feet, staring at him intently. Finally, Alex grinned and plucked a pancake off the stack.

"Radar, fetch!" he shouted, and flung the pancake across the room like a Frisbee.

"Alex!" his mother laughed, as Radar bounded across the room in two steps, caught the pancake in mid-air, and wolfed it down in a single gulp.

"He likes your cooking, honey," said their dad.

She threw him a fake angry look but still enjoyed the compliment. She turned to Alex.

"So is there something you'd like to do special for your birthday-plus-one?"

Alex thought about it a long time. He thought about airplanes and video games, pizza and baseball, cupcakes and the Yankees.

"Yeah," he answered. He knew exactly what he wanted to do.

Alex's dad found a parking spot in front of the burned-out lot at 417 Van Orton Street. As they all got out of the car, Mac appeared on his front porch, looking tired and suspicious. But it was just like before: as soon as he saw Alex and Nunu and Radar, his face opened up, and a kind old man smiled out.

Alex led the way through the front gate, carrying a plastic food container under his arm. Mac bent down and gave him a big hug, then stood back up as Alex introduced his parents. Alex's dad put both hands around Mac's when he shook his hand.

"Thank you for taking care of them," his dad said quietly.

"It was my pleasure," Mac smiled.

Mac led the way inside. Nunu introduced them to Dottie and flopped down on the sofa beside her to watch cartoons.

"I'll go put on a pot of coffee," said Mac.

Alex stepped forward. "I'll help," he said. His parents hung back; they knew he wanted a moment alone with Mac.

Alex led Mac into the kitchen. "I wanted to give you this first," he said, and opened the food container.

Inside was a big piece of his birthday cake. The green icing on top read "–Dawg."

"I saved you a piece," said Alex.

Mac nodded and got very quiet.

"What say we share?" he said, opening a drawer and taking out two forks.

Alex put up his hand. "Wait."

He pulled two birthday candles out of his pocket and stood them up on the cake, side-by-side. Then he found the matches his dad had loaned him, struck one carefully, and held it to the first bare wick.

"Better to light a candle," Alex said.

Mac looked at Alex in surprised recognition, then broke into a wide, gentle smile, his eyes dancing in the warm glow of the flickering flames.

ACKNOWLEDGMENTS

A writer is only as good as his team, and it was my great fortune to have the estimable Jennifer Flannery in my corner. As both agent and patient editor, she never lost belief in this story and poured countless hours (and buckets of red ink) into trimming and shaping and hacking away the chaff. There is no way to repay her contribution other than with my deep and heartfelt thanks.

My friend and agent Sandy Weinberg deserves credit and a big hug for pushing me to write a story about 9/11 from a kid's perspective. His support and encouragement were unflagging and essential.

To everyday hero Jeff Shapiro and his students at McKinley Avenue School in Los Angeles, a huge thank you for being my very first (and very enthusiastic) test audience. Go Tigers!

Robert Kuhn, Sheila Barnes, and Mary Ann Barnes get a big thank you for the excellent input on early drafts and for the reminders not to make Alex a jerk. Great advice from great writers.

To Mary Ann Key, director and founder of Key School in Ft. Worth: thank you not only for your invaluable feedback and guidance on how this book might be used as a teaching tool but also for your lifelong devotion to your (very lucky) students.

To teacher Lori Key and her young writers (Alinnah, Min, and Sabrina) at the Western Academy of Beijing: your enthusiasm for the novel and feedback on the cover gave me the boost I needed to get to the finish line. *Xie xie!*

Many thanks to author Scotty-Miguel Sandoe for generously sharing his wisdom and for reminding me to be quiet because the tables have ears.

Deepest gratitude to cover designer Tim Kordik for capturing a book full of words in a single image, to website designer Caryl Butterloy for turning a web page into a journey, and to photographer Minh Pham for not turning to stone when I smiled.

To my parents, Cullen and Dolores: no son could have asked for better. Not even Alex.

Finally (hide your eyes, kids): a big, sloppy kiss to my wife, Jennifer. We did it, monkey.

ABOUT THE AUTHOR

Tom Rogers is a novelist and the screenwriter of numerous animated films, including *The Lion King 1½, Kronk's New Groove, LEGO: The Adventures of Clutch Powers,* and Disney's *Secret of the Wings*. Originally from Texas, he now lives in Los Angeles with his wife, Jennifer. *Eleven* is his first novel for young adults.

Minh Q. Pham